I0829558

"One day I wondered:
what if elephants had been
first on the moon and taken
control of the world?"

Published by Basic Shapes Publishing
Elizabeth Bay Australia
basicshapespublishing@gmail.com

Copyright © Eileen Kramer 2021
eileen-kramer.com

All rights reserved. No part of this publication may be reproduced, stored in a retrieval system, or transmitted in any form or any means electronic, mechanical, photocopying, recording or otherwise without the prior permission of the publisher.

Every attempt has been made to locate the copyright holders for material quoted or images printed in this book. Any person or organisation that may have been overlooked or misattributed may contact the publisher for correction in any future printing.

Editing, design and layout: Catherine Gray
Cover image: Detail of self-portrait by Eileen Kramer, submitted for the Art Gallery of NSW's Archibald Prize in 2019.

ISBN: 978-0-6451943-0-2

A catalogue record for this work is available from the National Library of Australia

Elephants
& other stories

Eileen Kramer

Basic Shapes Publishing
2021

Foreword

I speak to EK most days. Conversation is pithy, focused and always, without fail, concerned with her next creative act – a story, a drawing, a costume, or a dance drama. There are a few of us who facilitate this, but she is in the driver's seat, in complete control.

At the beginning of 2020, when we had just finished filming Eileen's new choreography, the world began to shut down. She went into COVID lockdown in much the same way as she tackles life – with elegance and creative gusto – and instead of retreating and succumbing to woes of enforced isolation, she went to work.

While the world shuddered on, battling the virus, Eileen and editor Cathy Gray (who Eileen had fortuitously met through Lulworth House) wrote these stories. And as the lockdown lengthened, Eileen's remarkable memory and imagination went into overdrive. Mid-winter, mid-lockdown, she told me that this was probably the most enjoyable, creative time of her life.

Why was I not surprised? As a choreographer, I'm fascinated by the histories our bodies possess, with layer upon layer of experience adding depth and richness as time passes. This makes Eileen a veritable treasure trove. In her inimitable style, she re-writes the rules for centenarian behaviour and blows apart our cultural mindset that dance (and most things) are only for the young. She is a true dancing spirit and living proof of the value of creativity for a healthy and long life.

The stories in this book attest to both the spirit that has animated her for 106 years and her quirky yet acute powers of observation. They celebrate the small moments in a life – whimsical, everyday happenings that, if looked at in the right light, dance with magic.

Sue Healey
October 2020

Contents

"I write not only about what happened,
but also what comes to my mind...
In my stories people can fly
and change shape and do other
unusual or extraordinary things."

Part 1:
People & animals

The bees

There were two houses. The south-facing one was large, with seventeen rooms; the smaller one, with five rooms, faced the Yankees in the north. The two were separated by a mini-forest with a path running through it from house to house.

When Carli came to live with Bill, who owned the large house and the forest, she fell in love with the little house. Everyone who walked past it used to say, I wonder who lives in that house. No one knew.

Carli loved living with Bill in the grand house but she found the little house romantic and a bit magical. It made her think of Grimm's fairy tales. Once she had discovered it on the edge of the forest, she walked the path often, and the path became more and more defined as a result. She never entered the building, for the doors were always locked. But she swore she sometimes saw a woman's face at an upstairs window. For some reason she didn't tell Bill about it.

On one of her walks along the path, she found herself surrounded by bees. They buzzed busily all around her, so she imagined there must be a hive. While she was wondering about this, a man's head and shoulders began to rise through a hole in the ground near her feet. After all of him had stepped out and bowed to her, he told her that the name by which he was known was Mr B — the beekeeper.

"I'm French," he said.

Carli felt obliged to say, "Enchanté, Monsieur B. Comment allez-vous?" but she didn't quite believe him. Being French didn't explain his appearance from a hole in the ground.

The bees gathered around him. He said, "A bientôt," and led the swarm into the hole and away to wherever they lived below the surface. Carli continued her walk trying to understand what had just happened.

It was several days later that she saw Mr B again. The bees were there too but they were quiet and moving about slowly. Mr B was lying on the ground. He looked like a dead man, but Carli knew he was just pretending.

Just as she was about to move away and go on with her walk, she saw a young boy coming through the trees with his mother. When the boy saw Mr B he said, "Look mum, there's Mr B. He looks dead, doesn't he. But he's pretending — I saw him move."

Without opening his eyes Mr B muttered angrily, "Moved, did I? Well, that's that."

The boy's mother said, "Now you've upset him. Go on home and don't forget to wash your hands and face before your dad gets home. I'll be along later."

She turned and went off one way and the boy went the other. Neither of them used the path. They went through the trees.

Almost instantly another boy came along with an older sister. "Look sis," he said. "There's Mr B. He's pretending to be dead but I saw him breathe."

"Saw me breathe, did ya?" Mr B said angrily. "I am dead and I like it − no one to tell me to do anything." He made a rude noise in French and slapped at a bee that happened to fly slowly past. "That's that," he said.

The boy and his sister moved on, but then yet another boy came upon the scene, this time with his uncle. The boy pointed in the direction of Mr B and said, "Look Uncle Albert, that's Mr B. He's supposed to be dead. He likes it I think; he's a bit touched − the elevator isn't going all the way to the top."

"A bit touched, am I?" said Mr B. "I'll be dead if I like and I do like. You're too young to understand. I want to be dead and that's that." He added another rude word in French, which Carli understood.

That evening she told Bill about Mr B and all the strangers walking through the forest. He laughed and said, "I've got forty-five cousins in West Virginia alone. You should be thankful they don't all want to come and live with us."

No further explanation.

She went back the next day. Mr B looked wild-eyed and said he and the bees were very upset because the queen bee was missing − had been for two days. The bees themselves looked almost lifeless.

Carli said, "But that's not possible." She had an idea that queen bees didn't fly. She had thought they stayed in their room or cell or whatever giving birth to keep the hive alive.

Mr B just nodded distractedly and would say no more except, "That's what you think, mademoiselle. Strange things can happen and this isn't your average queen. Go away. Go over to that old house you think is so romantic and see what's going on there."

Carli said, "Why don't you go and look for her?"

"Mon dieu," said Mr B. "That's not my place. I'd only make things worse. She's after something I can't give her. Go and look for your silly cat that's been missing for a day."

Carli felt alarmed. It was true. Her cat had gone missing again. Normally she didn't worry about Nelly as she usually came back after one of her long outings. Supposing ... but she didn't know what to suppose.

She went on to the little house and this time she found the back door had been unlocked. There was a faint smell of honey in the air.

She would have gone in to explore the whole five rooms, had she not seen Nelly's tail disappearing though the trees. She went after her, calling, "Nelly, Nell, where are you?" But Nelly had gone off again.

It was time for dinner, so she went back home to make blueberry pie for Bill. She was still a bit worried about Nelly, and hoped the cat hadn't done something bad to the queen bee. As they ate dinner, she asked Bill, "Did anyone ever live in the little house?"

Bill didn't answer, he just looked a mite strange. She felt there was something she shouldn't ask about the house. Bill didn't tell her everything; she didn't ask. They each had their own thoughts that they kept to themselves. Which kept their relationship interesting and exciting.

Anyway, Nelly came back so that was all right, except she had some sticky stuff on her back legs that she kept trying to lick off.

That night, as Carli lay in the wide double bed in the spacious room she had all to herself, she heard a faint cry. She tried to tell herself it was just some animal on the prowl. Then she heard it again and knew it wasn't that at all – even though it was a strange kind of sound. Before she could do anything about it – and what could she have done anyway? – she fell asleep.

At breakfast the next morning she told Bill. "It sounded like someone was in trouble," she said. To her surprise, Bill looked at her seriously. He hardly ever did. This time he said, "It's happened again. Better go and find out."

He got his car and said, "I'll drive around by the house and you come up behind it." He meant: go through the woods and look that way.

Just as she came out of the woods, she saw Bill's car and called out to him. She knew where last night's cry had come from – inside the house itself.

Together they entered by the back door, looking around the downstairs rooms – no one there. They mounted the stairs, looked into the first bedroom – no one. Only one room left. And there they saw a distressing sight – certainly distressing for the poor lady who they'd never seen before.

She was beautiful, with long golden hair wound about her shoulders. She wore a diaphanous cloak that made Carli think, "Oh her wings are folded." She must have been trying to push the window either up or down, but it had slipped – perhaps the sash cord had broken – and captured both her hands at the wrists.

How long had she been in that predicament? Carli blamed herself, as she remembered the cry in the night.

Bill lifted up the window to free her and Carli stood behind her in case she would lose her balance and stagger back. Bill told her his name and began to introduce Carli.

"I know who you are," she replied. She brushed past them and ran down the stairs, leaving behind a faint trail of yellow dust and a smear of gold on the window.

They followed, but by the time they got downstairs she was nowhere to be seen. And they never saw her again.

The next day, when Carli went along the path, she found Mr B in a wonderfully good mood. The queen had returned. Ψ

Illustration: Eileen Kramer in 'Fragments of Sappho', Lewisburg Spring Concert, 2012; choreography and costume design by Eileen. Drawing by Eileen (detail).

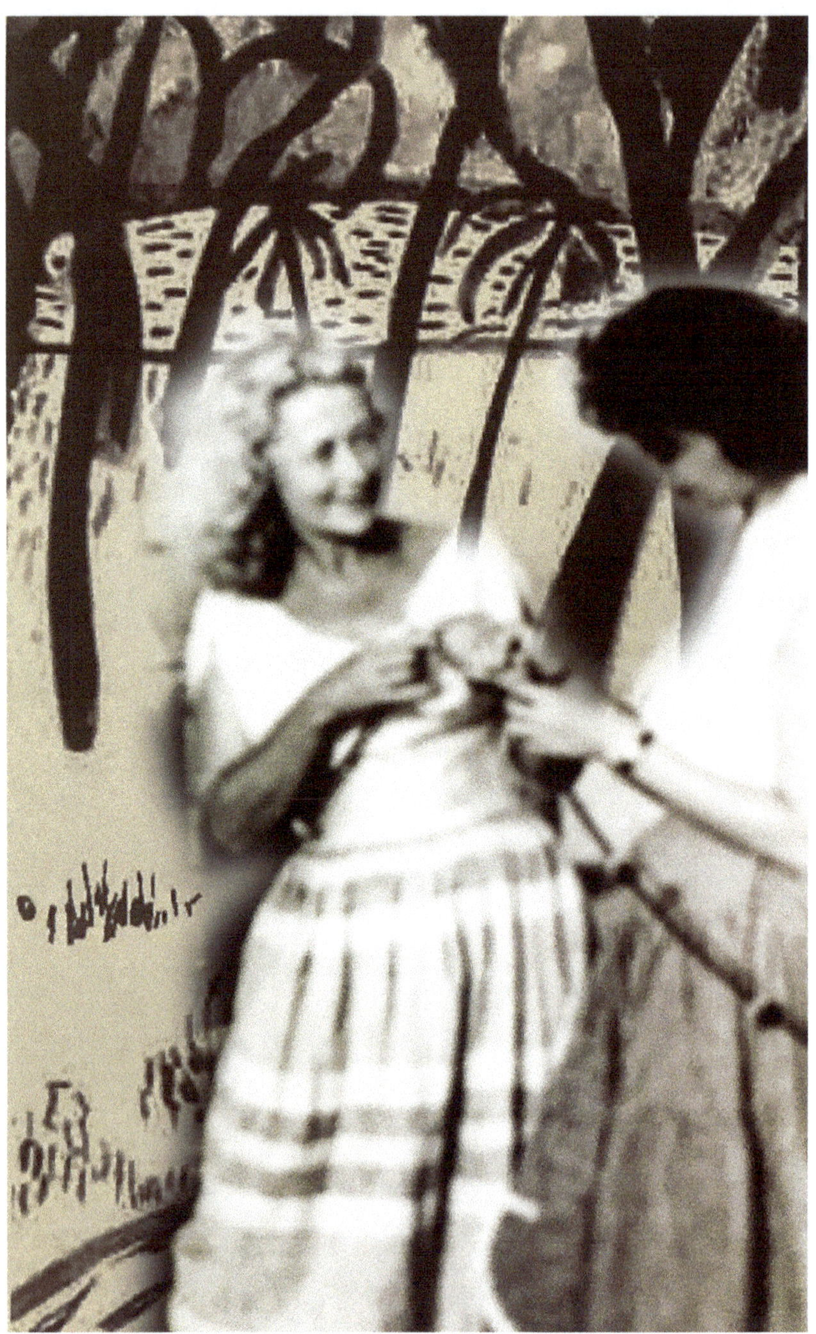

The earthworm

I had never thought of Moira as an earth mother, although some people might have seen her that way, because she was the daughter of official nudists. Her father and mother had been members of a nudist organisation in England. Having experienced England during a very cold winter, I had trouble envisaging such a thing. No wonder they came to Australia to pursue their dream of a life of healthy and beautiful nudity.

Moira's father, Kleber Claux, was a large handsome Frenchman. He had a fulsome beard and what I considered romantically untidy hair. He sold organic fruit and vegetables from his barrow on Liverpool Street, Sydney. No one looked down on that, and he won my heart when he came backstage after one of our dance concerts and complimented me on what he called my 'lovely leetel voice'. I had performed my Indian love song, in which I had to dance and express a poem by one of India's great poets, Rabindranath Tagore. M. Claux's accent as he said the work 'leetel' was really charming. I'd not expected that of Moira's father, Moira being so Australian.

Moira's mother was English. Somehow she surprised me by her typical motherliness. I couldn't imagine her without clothes. Moira showed me a photo of her as a young lady, wearing a particularly fine georgette dress. When Moira, who had studied dance in Madame Bodenwieser's school on Pitt Street in Sydney ever since the age of six, was to join the company, her mother came to talk to Madame, very seriously, about what kind of suitcase she should buy for Moira to take on tour.

At that time, sexual freedom was forbidden, of course, for everyone except the Claux family, and Moira began having boyfriends quite early. So it was a little surprising when, a few years later, Moira and the son of well known artist settled down and had children. Madame wasn't very pleased because Moira, by now a strong dancer, lived with her partner and her three children in a distant suburb of Sydney too far away for her to come to class and rehearsals. I think Madame was secretly pleased when the father of Moira's children left her, and she moved back to be near us and re-join the company.

When at last Moira found a good man, they married and eventually built a very modern house in a suburb of Brisbane.

Much later, after her husband had died, Moira invited me to visit her there. She cooked a very Australian dinner for me, and I spent the night in a good-sized double bed. Next morning, we had a typical bacon and egg breakfast.

Moira then took me into her back garden. I expressed my amazement, never having seen her as a gardener. Then she showed me a wooden box with some earth in it and a lot of wriggling and writhing worms she said she had purchased. I was indeed surprised: I had never imagined one could buy earthworms!

Over our 11 o'clock morning tea I told my friend about my only other experience of earthworms – such marvels of nature and evolution.

One summer, I said, I was travelling by car in France with a companion called Jane. We had been driving all through France together and were on our way south to the Côte d'Azur. We were on a long hot road when we came across a small general store – the only one for miles. And Jane, who was driving, stopped the car so that I could go across and see if I could buy some lemon or orange drink.

I left Jane sitting in the car in the shade of a tree, and over the road I went.

Inside the store, I managed to find a bottle of some sort of French lemonade, paid for it and turned back to the car. The road was very hot, I must say. Looking down at its hot black surface, what did I see but an earthworm, all pinkish and longish, making its way to the side of the road.

I bent over, watching it, intrigued as a dancer by its movements. I had never seen such a thing before. The front part of its body extended, getting thinner as it went. Then the middle section, which had been drawn together so that it looked rounded and fat, went forward to fill up, as it were, the front thin section. Having done that the last section was pulled up so that it too became fat and rounded. The front section then went forward, becoming long and thin again, and the middle and last parts repeated their movements.

Awed and fascinated, in a kind of scientific exultation, I

didn't move, wanting more and more of nature's wonder.

Then I realised that the poor creature had to reach the soft earth at the side of the road before it got itself fried on the hot surface of the bitumen. I ran to the side, picked up the softest leaf I could find, and hurried back.

The worm took advantage of this blessing, got busy with its front, middle and rear sections, and slid aboard the leaf. I picked it up and carried my treasure of nature to safety, where it soon disappeared into the earth to continue its day's work.

I went back to the car, and we opened the bottle of lemonade and quenched our thirst.

"What were you doing?" Jane asked, "bending over the road like that."

"I was saving the life of an earthworm," I replied.

Jane, who was often delighted but never surprised by anything, said "Oh, that's what you were doing. Alright. Let's go."

She started the car and on we went to the Côte d'Azur.

That's the way a story goes sometimes. You start by speaking about one thing, and find at the end that your tale has been about something else. Ψ

Illustration: Eileen and friend on the island of Crete, 1962? Background from painting 'Forest on the way to Goa' by Eileen Kramer (see also 'The tiger', page 69).

15

16

A sad monkey

This is a story of a very sad monkey, but it doesn't begin with him, for I first have to tell you about my friend Percival.

When we of the Bodenwieser dance company were on tour in Australia, we gave a concert in Brisbane. The Bodenwieser company had come from Vienna, Austria, and our style was different from classical ballet in that we danced with bare feet, not ballet toe shoes. There were other differences but there's no reason for me to go into them here.

After the performance in Brisbane, Madame Bodenwieser came to the dressing room. She looked coy in the old central European way, and said there was a young man in the audience who would like to meet the two waterlilies – Jean and myself. This was Percival.

It was unusual for Madame to make such an introduction. She did not like us to go out with men after a performance. I mention this because Percival, as it turned out, had a wonderful quality of being able to go in anywhere and be accepted by whomever to such an extent that he eventually made a name for himself in the fashion world in Paris.

At the time I met him, he was known as Don Savage, and he was to become my great friend.

After spending some time in Sydney working mostly as an extra in the opera company, Don decided to go to

London to 'seek his fortune', as they say of people like Dick Whittington and his cat. Don didn't have a cat, but he had a parrot who could say a few cheeky things. Don took a job on a cargo ship sailing from Adelaide – a lowly sort of job but one that would get him where he wanted to go.

He was told to report for duty on a certain evening to start work before the ship sailed. After travelling all the way from Sydney he arrived at the port and found the ship just as a bad storm blew up.

Once on board he saw everyone was very busy doing things to keep the ship safe. Unable to find anyone to report to, he lifted a tarpaulin covering one of the lifeboats, scrambled inside with his meagre luggage, and eventually went to sleep.

He woke up about three hours later, when the ship was far out at sea, and waited to be told his duties. But as it happened, in the storm he had gone aboard the wrong ship. It was too late to turn back, so Don was carried on, and by the time he got to England he had taught the crew the Indian dance from *Annie Get Your Gun* and become friends with everyone, including the captain.

He went ashore in London, but after a day and a half he returned to tell the captain that he didn't like London, so they carried him on to the next port in France. From there he went on to Paris and eventually got a job on an English-speaking newspaper.

That was the beginning of a successful career as a public relations man for the great French fashion houses.

Don Savage became Percival Sauvage. He got to know everyone who was famous and became famous himself. His was the name that inspired Dior's famous perfume Eau Sauvage.

The parrot, his faithful companion, had long ago been given to a man who liked parrots.

When I reached Paris myself, by more conventional means, I found Percival and he helped me find somewhere to live, saw to it that I was dressed in models from the Summer Collections of Lanvin, and took me shopping and to cafes and bistros and parties.

It was at a flea market that we came upon the sad monkey.

Percival – which I learned to say in the correct French way, 'pear-see-vaal' – had, by the way, an apartment on the Left Bank that he let me use when once he had broken a small bone in his foot and couldn't manage the stairs. I was not yet the owner of my own flat. Percival was very kind to me, and also to other Australians who came to Paris.

Anyway, on this day, we were strolling through the flea market, not expecting to see anything unusual. We saw many things we would have liked to buy; some we did purchase, some we did not.

Then we came upon a cage in which a monkey sat quietly looking so very sad and lonely. Imagine – he was for sale!

When Percival touched the side of the cage, the monkey reached out with his soft and delicate paw and pulled very gently on Percival's arm, as if to say, "Please take me and get me out of here."

Now, what would we have done with a monkey? We longed to be able to take him, but how could we keep him?

We had to leave, and as we walked away, we looked back and saw his sad monkey eyes still pleading with us to take him away from all the people who saw him only as an object of curiosity.

How bad we felt — how selfish and even cruel. We knew we would lie awake in our beds that night, thinking of him.

The next day, as if by some wonderful design of fate, two of Percival's friends — people of the kind he knew so well — came to Maison Lanvin with the intention of looking at gowns like the one with which Percival had robed me and which had so delighted me. She, the elegant and eccentric wife, had come to find one for herself. Her husband, also eccentric and quite rich, was to buy it for her.

They called on Percival to tell him what they were doing, and I — also by fate — was with Percival in his office.

Percival and I looked at each other, knowing each other's thoughts. Here was the answer! Not only would they purchase the incredibly expensive gown for madame, but they would buy a monkey as well.

We had to explain this to them straight away.

Promising to come back that very day for the model gown, these two eager people, along with Percival and me, went in their Rolls Royce to the market, found the cage, bought the monkey and took him back to Lanvin with us, for the hour was late by now.

That evening, at a fine, very French dinner at the home

of Percival's rich friends, we saluted the monkey, to whom we gave the name Baudelaire. He of course couldn't fully understand what was going on, but he no longer looked sad.

Before the week had passed, Baudelaire was given his own enclosure in the garden of the rich friends, with all he seemed to need to make him happy, and furthermore, a lady monkey to make him even happier. She and Baudelaire fell in love, and that made us happy too, for it could have turned out disastrously if they had not liked each other at all.

But no, everything was très formidable. Ψ

Illustration: 'The small wet monkey' (Tatiana Morozova/Alamy Stock Photo), and 'The Paris Hat' (print by Robert Dickerson, 1999; courtesy of the estate of Robert Dickerson). 'Room 8', on page 171, tells the story of how Eileen came across the Dickerson work.

The goat

'Them lesbeens' was how the woman down the creek referred to us. That wasn't quite true but Maryat didn't mind.

Fran said, "I didn't meet a good man, so I met a good woman." We presumed she meant Maryat because they shared the main bedroom. Otherwise, they didn't flaunt their relationship.

That summer, I had been given the next best bedroom, as a guest. The twenty young people of the Governor's Summer Youth Program mostly lived close by with their parents.

Maryat owned two other houses, including a cabin up the hill, and she had recently purchased two wide fields. There was also a barn used as a rehearsal space by the theatre group she had founded. The plays she wrote and directed for the Eco Theatre were mostly to do with the people of the old railroad days, when the train depot was in Hinton, not far from Powley's Creek. The creek ran down from the mountain, which wasn't a very high one, past the properties of the four or five local families, along the side of the road and through a short tunnel, until it flowed into the river.

There were no animals on Maryat's property at first, except one young bull who always came to the fence to have his head scratched. But once she was well established and had called her place the Women's Farm, Maryat bought some chickens and a goat.

The goat wasn't an old billygoat with a wispy beard and tufts of food hanging out of his mouth. He was a goat of another sort. To my eyes he looked pretty and poetic, like something out of a tale by Hans Christian Anderson. He was so graceful and gently behaved that, knowing Maryat, I wondered whether she had bought him as a slightly ironic symbol of the Women's Farm.

After a while, nobody took much notice of him except me. He and I became friendly and we had our picture taken together.

I think I made such a friend of the goat because we both felt a bit like outsiders. Maryat and Fran felt that way too. We weren't West Virginians like everyone else, and Fran had the additional strangeness of being Jewish. Maryat told me she had been in Powley's Creek for two years before one of her neighbours up the hill, Mr Buckland, had called her one afternoon and said, "You better close up tight tonight Mizzz Lee. There's gonna be a big storm." She had finally been accepted.

That wasn't to say that Mr Buckland hadn't on another occasion encountered Maryat in her barn and put his arm around her, saying, "Now Mizzz Lee, we're both grow'd up … etc etc." To which Maryat had replied in very firm tones, "Mr Buckland! Take your hands off me this minute." He did so, and Mr and Mrs Buckland ended up becoming her best friends on Powley's Creek.

That summer when I was visiting Maryat at the Women's Farm, the first of the Eco Theatre plays we performed was about John Henry, the legendary black tunnel digger who had been immortalised in folksong.

A girl called Kathy Jackson played the role of John Henry, and the young people from the Governor's Summer Youth Program played the tunnel diggers and work gangs of the Chesapeake Railroad. The rhythm of their singing echoed the rhythm of their movements as they dug and lifted and placed the rails.

I was in that play as a lady called Mourning Glory, who danced at the tunnel entrance for the wives waiting for their menfolk to emerge from the dark hole in the side of the mountain. It wasn't my kind of dance, not my kind of thing at all, but Maryat wanted me to do it, so I did. Later, when the trouble began, I rather wished I hadn't.

However, the trouble hadn't started yet and we all had fun in the beginning, especially when we went out on short day tours. I learned a lot about West Virginians and about the countryside itself.

The goat had nothing to do with John Henry or the tunnel or the plays. His duty was to impart an air of romance to the field of small white flowers next to Maryat's house. He did it very well. I had a feeling he knew that. He posed well for the photos.

That was a lovely summer, even though I had felt a little out of it.

The next summer came, and Maryat asked me to do my dance at the entrance again in the John Henry play. So I said I would.

Things weren't going as well as the first time. For one thing, Fran had fallen in love with a visitor to West Virginia. She still had to spend her time working on the Eco Theatre plays, which made her grumpy: she couldn't run off to join her new girlfriend whenever she wanted to.

Maryat herself was not well. It was her heart, and the doctor in Hinton ordered her to go to hospital. She was to leave us to undergo some dangerous procedure.

Being Maryat, she made the most of the drama. The day she was leaving she called a meeting in the large kitchen/dining room to tell us how we should manage while she was away. There were four young interns from the University of West Virginia staying in one of Maryat's other houses that month, and they came to the meeting too.

We all – Fran, the interns and myself – waited for Maryat to make her appearance. When she did, she placed a pile of papers on the table and after a dramatic pause, spoke very seriously, looking at each one of us in turn. "Well, it's been good," she said. Obviously, she meant 'life': life had been good to Maryat. Fran looked a bit doubtful, for she hadn't been pleased with life lately, and the interns, believing her, looked a bit concerned. Only I and my friend the goat, who had wandered in after me, saw how Maryat had staged the scene.

The meeting started soberly enough, but as it went on the drama turned to comedy, with everyone offering increasingly outrageous solutions to Maryat's predicament.

Well, she went off, with Fran driving, not to the local

hospital but to the one in Charleston, several hours away.

Once we were left on our own, bedlam broke loose. Cars came to and fro during the night; rehearsals went badly; people began pairing off. One of the Summer Program girls openly began a love affair with one of the interns. Only a few days later – I mean, too early to be sure – she said she feared she may be pregnant. Then it all came out: her proud and strict black grandfather would kill the intern. Others, both black and white, became rebellious and refused to continue with John Henry. Gracie, the cat, got killed by one of the neighbour's dogs. The Summer Program young people turned on me as an outsider and said they'd leave the project, threatening to come to the performance and throw ripe, wet tomatoes at me. One of the interns defended me, saying he'd stand in front of me and suffer the blows. The young people laughed and said they would not be arrested because they were too young. The goat and I continued to pose in the field of flowers.

Fran came back and said Maryat hadn't died and would probably be home within two days.

More cars roared up and down the valley in the night and Emily, the neighbour's daughter, one of the Summer Program girls, stood up defiantly and said she was going to become a 'lesbeen'. She wanted me to give her the man's vest I had made as part of her overseer's costume.

All the emotion brought things to a climax. To make matters worse, John, the most reliable and theatrically serious of all the interns, was stung by a bee and had to be taken to hospital because he was allergic to bees and could die that night if not attended to.

At this point, Maryat's mother arrived, a former southern belle who'd married into the family of General Robert E Lee.

Fran said, "She isn't going to sleep on Maryat's side of the bed with me." So I had to give up my second-best bedroom and move to a little room up the back of the house.

Maryat came home safe, but that summer, in a way, was the end of the Eco Theatre. Fran left Maryat eventually and went to live in the nearby town of Lewisburg. Maryat sold the Women's Farm and she too went to Lewisburg, where she had bought an old house.

They might have felt they had failed, and become depressed. But it was not really the end for anyone, even the young people of the Governor's Summer Youth Program.

Maryat went on with her dream in a different way. She gathered the young people together again and taught them to write and direct their own plays as well as act in them. These plays were genuine and heart-felt. There was one about a house that felt lonely because no one lived in it, and another about waiting for a cousin to come back from the war in Vietnam. But it wasn't just the plays that mattered. One day, about 12 months later, I came across one of the Youth Program girls working at the checkout in the Lewisburg supermarket. She had been the kind of girl to hide her face; now she stood tall. "Did Eco Theatre make a difference to you?" I asked her. "Yes," she said. "Just look at me."

Fran built a modern house on a hill just outside Lewisburg, with the aid of just one man. It had a large studio and performance space, with a big wide verandah around it. She became a professional musician — a pianist — and taught and gave concerts. She found herself a good woman, or several. But that didn't stop her occasionally standing outside Maryat's place and telling her loudly to "Clean your house!"

I went back to New York, where Maryat generously lent me an apartment on condition that I write 30 pages of stories a week and send them to her for comment. It was hard work but I did it. I got some good stories out of it.

Maryat and Fran remained friends until they died: Maryat first — she was standing at her computer when her heart finally gave out — and then Fran, many years later.

I imagine that Maryat's brother, named after their famous ancestor Robert E Lee, inherited the house — and the goat. I couldn't keep him where I lived, so regrettably I had to leave him behind. Ψ

Illustration: Eileen and the goat; photo from Eileen's collection, West Virginia, 1980s.

The camels

Imagine a large dray with a crowd of people sitting back-to-back or cross-legged or somehow finding space for themselves, all being taken somewhere – by a camel.

Or imagine a camel race in Alice Springs. Or a camel making its way along Pitt Street or Bourke Street in the rush hour.

Imagine a camel looking cranky – they often do look cranky.

They're funny animals, camels. Tony Curtis and Jack Lemon dressed as girls in *Some Like It Hot* were funny. I really laughed at them, and am sorry they don't exist any more. Who's taken their place? The series *Seinfeld* had a character called 'Kramer' who I thought was funny but I mainly liked him because Kramer is my second name.

Getting back to camels: the ones in this story didn't have full bodies, just heads and necks and humps made of paper and glue, on long sticks, with a kind of skirt where their legs would have been. They had a rather cross look and took themselves very seriously, hardly realising that they had no lower parts.

They were 'props' I made for a dance drama about the wife of Prince Siddhartha, who afterwards became the Buddha. In the scene, the camel train enters with the young Princess Bulbul in a golden robe. Everyone else, including the camels, was wearing striped costumes. It's funny how stripes are always used for desert scenes, even though most Arabs in deserts wear a plain kaftan and head scarf. But that's theatre for you. And I liked the strong black and white fabric I had found in the local shop.

When the season was over, all the costumes were stored, and the camels went with them. They were even crosser than usual. "We're no use to anyone in here," they grumbled to each other. In the storeroom they rose up above everything else, on their long wooden poles. Like the "yellow god forever gazing down" as the poem went – but that's another Indian story.

Then a man named Chally Erb came along. Chally had just returned from California, where he had been studying contemporary mime. He hadn't liked the Trillium company at first, but as he began to have more success with his mime pieces he became more involved with us. Our audiences loved him.

Anyway, Chally had started working on a new piece that had something to do with Egypt and the Nile. As always, one idea gave birth to another and Chally visualised a scene with my camels, even though they had no lower body or legs.

The camels, of course, were excited. "On stage again!" they muttered.

Chally tidied them up and had new skirts made for them. I didn't mind that. I liked what he was doing with them. It was good to see them coming to life again. He had other characters of early Egypt as well, such as the sphinx and a few pyramids, and even water of the Nile.

Chally's piece was successful, and the camels got quite a lot of press coverage. I think it rather shocked them.

"We really only want to work for you and Chally," they said.

But Chally's next mime piece didn't include camels and neither did my new dance drama, which was about Isis and Osiris. So I was concerned about my camel friends. That's what they had become. They had served me — or rather my dance work — well and that made me care about them. Chally and I were speaking about this one day, and we came up with a good solution.

"Supposing we had a nice glass house made for them to live in until the day we might need them again," I said to Chally. "We could keep it in the lobby of the theatre so they'd have the feeling they were still wanted. They really love performing just as much as we do."

I looked at him. "We're just a couple of show-offs, aren't we," I added. "Well, they are too."

Chally agreed. "A great idea," he said.

So we did that.

Their house wasn't like an everyday suburban home. The effect was more like a room in an eastern palace. The camels loved it. Every now and then, without anybody noticing — even audiences milling about in the foyer — they would slowly and subtly change positions.

The mask of the lovely Princess Bulbul had agreed to join the camels in their glass room, posing with them just as she had done in her role in the drama. She said she was thrilled to be there, so audiences could see her again. We still had her golden robe — she was very pleased about that. And the camels wore the long striped skirts hiding their lack of legs.

The tableau in the foyer was a great success. It was also a reminder of the original *Buddha's Wife* dance drama, and that gave Chally another idea.

"Why not leave the door of the palace open?" he said. (He called their exotic glass case, a 'palace'.) His suggestion was that at night, if the camels desired, they could open the door and make their way in the faint light of the moon, with everyone sleeping (or so we hoped), to an area of desert sand left there no one knows why or how, and re-enact for their own pleasure the Princess's journey to Prince Siddharta's palace.

Maybe they did. One young man called Lester, from the mountain above Lewisburg, said he had seen something going on. He often stayed out late doing goodness knows what.

"I must be goin' mad," Lester told Chally. "I'd swear I saw a lotta camels dancin' out there on Arnold Fens' sand dune!"

"No you didn't," said Chally. "And if you go about sayin' so, we'll have you an' your horse banned from comin' into town!"

So, if anyone does happen to see the Princess Bulbul and her camel escort crossing the sand dunes late at night, just keep it to yourselves. Ψ

Illustration: Camel drawings by Eileen Kramer, and photo by Catherine Gray of a different dune, this one outside Birdsville in Queensland.

The cat

Jill and Ruben met in the countryside of southern France. They lived in a hotel on the Rue Delambre in Paris for a while, and came to New York at the height of independent movie-making fever. Ruben had studied film-making at New York University, so he soon felt the urge to make one himself.

First of all they had to get an apartment. Ruben was very good at things like that. While Jill waited at her friend Rachel's apartment on 6th Avenue down near Greenwich Village, Ruben went in search of a home for them. He was anxious to get started on his film.

He found fairly good accommodation up town a little. He had wanted something on Canal Street, where most of the filmmakers had their studios, but not finding anything there, he settled for an apartment on the tenth floor of a large building on East 91st Street. It wasn't far from the Museum of Art, so that was not bad.

He signed the contract without Jill's agreement, but fortunately she liked the apartment. Although it was furnished, she, who was very good at such things, soon made new bed covers and attractive cushion covers. They were happy about everything. Their home was all ready for them to live the life of a young newly married couple – the term 'partner' hadn't been taken up by people who wanted to live together without actually getting married. Ruben had said to her, "Jill, do you want to get married?" For some reason Jill had said no.

So that was that! But the first time Jill accompanied Ruben to the synagogue, he introduced her as his wife, and for as long as she went to the synagogue with him she was known as Mrs Feldhandler. Jill found this amusing. She thought it was fun to respond to the name 'Mrs Feldhandler'. So everything was fine. There was no child in their home, but Jill didn't mind that either.

Downstairs there was a room for tenants to store large suitcases and boxes and the like. It was a gloomy storage room with one small electric light, just enough to let you to find your own things. Jill wasn't afraid to go there, but she didn't venture further into the other dark and dismal rooms of the basement, which seemed to go on forever.

It was therefore a surprise when one day, while she was going through one of her suitcases, she heard a pathetic 'meow'. Looking into the darkness, she could just make out a tiny kitten crouched in the shadows. The little creature must have been so lonely it forgot to be frightened. It did not run away as most homeless cats would. It came straight to her arms, which she held out, full of warmth and comfort. How sweetly it snuggled its fragile body up against her chest. But she knew Ruben would say, "No cats," and mean it.

For three days she took food down to the basement, but the kitten had not yet learned how to eat. Jill smeared moist food onto her fingers and the kitten found out how to lick it off. On the fourth day, Jill picked up PussPuss, as she had called her, and took her home, climbing all ten flights of stairs because the elevator man wouldn't let the cat into his elevator.

To Jill's surprise, after one look Ruben fell completely in love and PussPuss fell for him too.

The filmmaking had already started. They were shooting an animated film in the old way, on 35mm film. It was called *The Pilgrimage of Truth*. The apartment was their studio, and all the sets and screens were made of materials Ruben found in the streets. PussPuss took part in everything that was going on. She enjoyed sliding across the floor on strips of slippery celluloid, and when a scene in a medieval castle was filmed, she loved walking under the cat-sized archways. She was with them all the way.

Jill and Ruben shared the creative work and for a long time making the film was their whole interest. But before it was finished, Ruben had a stroke and spent many months in hospital. It was not fatal – he eventually came home and the editing could begin.

It wasn't easy. Ruben suffered from anxiety, and would sometimes become angry or sulk, thinking his life was over. On those days, PussPuss would sit before him on the floor.

"Look at the cat," Jill would say. When he looked and felt the calm gaze of Pusspuss in return, Ruben's mood would pass and eventually he regained his mental strength.

Jill said Pusspuss was an angel living in their house. Without her, they agreed, the film would never have been finished.

But it was. And down on Canal Street when the other filmmakers were showing their sex-mad pictures or their abstract creations, Jill and Ruben's graceful morality tale was highly praised, especially the ending, where PussPuss's tail could clearly be seen crossing the castle drawbridge. Ψ

Illustration: PussPuss herself; background from drawing by Eileen Kramer (detail).

41

The skunk

On a long main road that passed through a small town in West Virginia, there was an odd-looking house.

It had been built by a woodworker for himself and his new wife to live in until the bigger house they had planned was ready for them. But the bigger house never got finished, so they went on living in the makeshift house for the rest of their lives.

After they died, the house was empty for many years and people walking past would say, "I wonder who lives in the little house?"

It inspired stories of a romantic nature. One young student wrote a short play about it. The story was that the house was lonely and full of hope that one day a family would make it their home, doing all the things that families do. It was a charming play – and original too, with young people acting the roles of the doors and walls and windows and so on.

To the great joy of the house, someone did at last really rent it, and settled into it. You can imagine the delight of the walls, windows and doors, and the staircase, made of particularly fine wood, and the back porch, with its lattice work and arched entrance. They were all very pleased with the new residents, a young woman called Ronnie Fiden and her husband Foster.

Ronnie felt happy there. She found a few precious things

that had belonged to the original owners – a vase, a rolling pin for rolling out pie crust and a scent bottle that still had some brown liquid that Foster said smelt like a Chinese brothel. How did he know? He got a smack for saying that! He'd never been further than Charleston, so who did he think he was saying things like that?

Still, she treasured it and never used it and eventually had to throw it out. She said the perfume should be called something worse, like skunk juice.

Skunks made their presence felt from time to time on Ronnie and Foster's land. Ronnie said she thought they lived out in the wild part of their grounds beyond the mown lawn – a large area of open land that Foster intended to make into a garden one day.

One day was a long time coming, so there it was, getting mowed every week, doing nothing, and all around it, other uncultivated land also doing nothing. Ronnie wanted vegetables – "them cabbages" – so she could can them against winter.

"And what about the squash and them beans you promised?"

Foster said he'd been busy.

"Oh yes, too busy to plant a few beans I suppose."

Still, they were happy enough.

The skunk smell got worse. Ronnie called the pest control. A young man came, said, "I'm pest control," and got a huge gun out of the back of his car. Ronnie was struck with dismay. "You're not going to shoot, it!" she cried in horror. The young man looked intensely relieved and said, "I don't want to. What if she's got young?" He put his gun away and drove off.

Well, summer came. The nights got warm, then hot. Foster hated the skunk smell but Ronnie would not let him do anything about it. In a strange way, she was getting used to it. It didn't keep her awake as it did Foster.

One day, he said he couldn't stand it any more. He was going up to his cousin Scooter's place for a few days, glad to get away from that awful stink.

Ronnie said she didn't want to go Scooter's place, with cows and bulls mooing and grunting loudly all day. "So I'll stay here and look after the place. Have a nice time and come back when you're ready."

Once he had gone, she felt strangely relieved. It wasn't that she didn't love him, but there was an eagerness in her to be alone with the warm summer night and its mysteries.

Later that evening, she got ready for bed, opened the window overlooking the wide moonlit landscape beyond the shed, and inhaled the midnight air. She opened her arms and breathed deeply, taking in the faint odour of the skunk, and with it, all of nature's fullness in the moment.

"Oh! I love it, I love it, I love it," she said. Ψ

Illustration: Montage of drawings by Eileen Kramer.

A lucky dog

When I learned, long after the event, that my grandmother had left my grandfather and a comfortable home on the North Shore to run away with a bricklayer named Mr Evans, it made me think of *Lady Chatterley's Lover*. My grandmother was quite happy with Mr Evans, who took her to live in a terrace house in Marrickville, and so was I. He was the only grandfather I ever knew.

Mr Evans and Grandma had a very pretty little dog named Flossie and this story is about something very terrible that almost happened to Flossie.

Every few months I would go and spend a few days in Marrickville with them. I went on Saturdays — a day when something quite *good* usually happened to Flossie. She would begin to get excited when Mr Evans ran a bath for her in the laundry room at the back of the house. She took the bath very well, even when she got soap in her eyes. Then after she had shaken all the water off and got dried, her excitement would mount. She would get a warm scone loaded with butter and so would Mr Evans and so would I, all made by Grandma in her kitchen. By this time, Flossie's excitement would reach a high peak: she knew what was coming next. After wiping all the butter off our faces, we would go for a walk, Mr Evans, Flossie and I. Mr Evans would get her leash, fasten her into it and off we would go.

They lived in a street off the main road. At the corner

was a shop that sold Catholic religious figures, like angels and saints. This shop interested me very much. The saints looked as though they were made of white plaster, painted in very lovely pastel shades of pink or blue with gold edges, and I think my love of long robes in my costume design comes from this experience.

Along the main street a little way was the bakery, and this part of the walk was more for me than Flossie or Mr Evans. When the baker's daughter, a girl my own age, was in the shop, she would put her hand into the glass case, take hold of a cream horn and give it to me. The woman who managed the shop didn't approve of this but I think the baker's daughter, whose name was Liz, was rather a spoilt child and could do what she liked.

After that, we would go further up the main street, where the buses rushed past us with great ferocity. We would then turn round and come back. Flossie was quite happy with this and would settle down at home.

One day, I don't know why but I went for a walk along the main street on my own. I had my eye on that cream horn but when I went into the shop, Liz was not there. The manager didn't even say hello. She just looked at me coldly and made no attempt to get the cream horn out of the glass case and give it to me.

So I came out onto the street again and walked slowly back towards the corner to have a look at the saints in their pink and blue costumes. Suddenly I heard a ferocious sound coming down the street. Looking around, I was horrified to see Flossie running along in front of a bus, wind streaming through her silky hair and a look of panic in her eyes. The bus driver was not taking any notice of her. The bus itself was rattling like an old tin can and at any moment, it was going run over poor Flossie. The poor dog couldn't run much faster than she was.

Just as she reached the corner, with the bus about to flatten her – squash her completely on the road – I yelled, 'Flossie!'

She heard me and at the last moment she leapt up into the air and sideways and landed in her own street. It was really quite remarkable how she did that. I never told Mr Evans or grandmother. They might have blamed me for letting Flossie out of the house, which I never did. **Ψ**

Illustration: Montage of drawings by Eileen Kramer.

A *feisty dog*

Tilly, Barbara's dog, had the strongest, loudest, most persistent bark I had ever heard.

I remember Barbara as a child. She was a student at Madame Bodenwieser's School of Dance when I was about twenty-five and already a member of the company. Now Barbara is quite grown up and has her own dance school.

When I returned to Sydney after a long time abroad I stayed with her in Paddington. I arrived at the front door having just flown in from America and Tilly was standing there in the hallway, barking excitedly and banging her tail against some piece of furniture. I was a little afraid of her. She was small with short hair that was wiry to the touch and altogether not at all an impressive-looking dog. I could see that Barbara was fond of her though, and while I lived with them I grew to like her too, in spite of myself.

I also believe that Tilly liked me. Sometimes she would sit on my lap. But if I walked within three feet of her while she was eating, she would bare her teeth and look at me as though I had come to steal her food. And this would continue until I was ten feet away. When it came to food, I was the enemy.

Barbara had given me a nice room with a good wide double bed, and I stayed for about four months with the two of them, Tilly and Barbara.

This was a little longer than Barbara had intended, I think. She told me to call an organisation called ACAT, to find some accommodation. So I did and a nice woman named Yolande came the next day with a colleague. Barbara took them into the parlour and wanted to serve tea, but no, they got out their iPads and did some thinking and talking and typing and then said they would come again tomorrow to take me to a place in Chippendale.

"Chippendale!" I said in horrified tones. "Who lives in Chippendale?"

Nevertheless they put me in a car with my luggage as well as a few cake spoons and forks and a cushion that Barbara gave me, saying "I think Eileen might like these". Tilly snarled and barked and off we went to an ex-pub in Chippendale called Thurles Castle.

Eventually, I moved out of there and found another place to stay, one that I liked very well, also in Chippendale. I visited Barbara and Tilly from time to time, and when I would ring the doorbell, Tilly would always be there, barking and growling and carrying on. Barbara would say, "Quiet Tilly; it's Eileen."

This always happened, even though we knew each other very well. How could a small dog manage to look so fearsome and make so much noise? But once I got inside you would have thought Tilly was madly in love with me. As before, she always wanted to sit on my lap, as though it was her rightful place.

When I was writing this story, I wondered where Barbara had got Tilly, so I called her to ask. She told me that Tilly was the daughter of a silky dog called Maisy, who escaped at the age of two and came back pregnant. Barbara adopted the puppy and their love affair began – and in a way my love affair too, although I had had my reservations, as I said to Barbara. "She was always like that," said Barbara, "It wasn't just you."

Then Barbara's voice changed, as though she had some momentous news for me. And it was so.

"Tilly died yesterday," she said. "She was old, blind, couldn't hear properly and didn't seem to be able to smell anything, so I called the vet and asked him to help Tilly onto her afterlife."

There I was, writing this little story about Tilly, and I hadn't expected that. It shocked me.

Later, as I was going to bed, I felt very sad. I even shed a tear for Tilly. I hadn't realised how fond of her I was. As Barbara said, she was a feisty little dog; she didn't try to make you like her. I wonder now how Barbara is faring without Tilly. Ψ

Illustration: Photo of Tilly as an old dog courtesy of Barbara Cuckson; background from drawing by Eileen (detail).

Dogs & cats

Maimuna, a girl from Karachi, went off to Italy to study art. Not long afterwards she fell in love with a successful young public relations man and got married to him. His name was Alberto, but she called him Bertie. Of course she stayed with Bertie in Milan, and in summertime they went to their villa in Gubbio, a sister town to Assisi.

Maimuna learned the language and as a wife she soon learned to please her husband – and also his relatives, who all seemed to share their charming villa at times.

In a way this was like her parents' home in Karachi. It was often not easy to know whose house it was in Karachi. Fortunately it was a large rambling kind of building. People could be hidden there and not found for days. On one occasion, a visitor noticed a young man alone with his rice bowl in a corner.

"Who is that?" the visitor asked.

"Oh," said Maimuna's beautiful mother, who was wearing the Muslim dress called shalwar kameez, which involved a romantic looking shawl. "I think he's someone who has run away from home. He can stay here until his parents, I hope, will come to get him."

Alberto and Maimuna's villa had a lawn where groups of people would sit on warm evenings, chewing on sunflower seeds and chatting. There was a shoulder-high stone wall all around, with an imposing wrought-iron gate. This was very useful later, when Maimuna began to take in runaway dogs and cats.

Inside the house was a smaller living room where people sometimes had coffee and conversation or listened to Italian love songs. One wall was completely taken up by a painting – a very naturalistic painting of another brick wall – which Maimuna had done at art school. It was enormous. Maimuna was actually not very fond of it because she felt its naturalistic style looked out of place in the villa. But there it was. Walls were rather the thing.

"Bertie paid a lot of money to have it brought from the school," she said, out of earshot of Alberto. "He likes it, so I keep it here."

In the summer we ate on the patio – I say 'we' for I, like the dogs and cats, was also a kind of runaway. We all sat at a long table, and once the food was put on it, we'd all tuck into the delicacies, pasta or cheese dishes.

At luncheon, everyone went a bit mad, shoving great dishes of pasta towards each other and shouting joyfully, "Mangia, mangia!" The dogs would also be running about, perhaps saying the same in dog language. It was quite exciting.

What a contrast, I thought, to luncheon at Patty Wideacre's place, where I had stayed before coming to Maimuna's. In her quiet way, Patty would ask for the cream to be passed to her. How could she bear to say it? I wondered. How could she bear the shame of everyone knowing she wanted cream on her strawberries?

Maimuna and Bertie had maybe four or five very nice dogs, I think – it was hard to tell how many exactly. They were all sizes and shapes, all perfectly at home. They had once been strays but word had got around that there was a great dog restaurant up at the villa and they had soon found a way in.

There were also cats – four of them – and that was where the walls came into the picture.

The dogs' food, specially cooked in a very big pot, would be ladled into the bowls with names on them. The dogs didn't discriminate about names, but neither did they did fight over their food; they all ate in gentlemanly style once they had settled before one bowl each.

The cats on the other hand had their food bowls arranged on top of the stone wall. They too knew their places and made no fuss. One little cat, when not on the wall, was constantly escaping from big human feet. She always made it to safety just in time.

There were limits – no dogs in the swimming pool, for instance! The pool, a little further down the slope, was Maimuna's creation. While we were enjoying the swimming and the diving and splashing about at one end, Maimuna would sit painting at the other, placidly and steadily transforming the walls of the pool into scenes from ancient Roman baths.

Alberto was really an adoring husband. When summer was over he and Maimuna would go back to Milan, leaving the animals in the care of a neighbour.

I had my doubts about this arrangement. Yet, when winter had passed and the iron gates of the villa were opened, there were the lovely dogs and cats, waiting for their food bowls on the tiled floor of the patio and on the wall. Maimuna took this for granted. She had no fears of them not being there.

A year later she sent me a photo of three of the dogs in a fan shape. I lost this somewhere, but I've drawn them for you, so you can see just how adorable they looked sitting together so politely. Ψ

Illustration: Drawing by Eileen Kramer, 2020.

The mouse

This is a very short story about how I saved the life of a mouse.

Living in a big old house with a lot of land, some cultivated and some not, I had to deal with all sorts of animals: squirrels in the ceiling; skunks, rabbits, even bears out in the woods; a family of loud crows. And two cats.

Strangely enough, I was never bothered by mice. Coming from Manhattan, I thought mice lived under the floorboards – possibly fighting it out with the cockroaches. But here, I never saw even one.

So I was a little surprised at what happened one rainy day when I came out of the kitchen into the back garden. I surprised myself in fact, with my own swift action in dealing with the situation.

That day I had been trying to stop the squirrels making such a racket in the ceiling – I say 'trying' because I never succeeded in making them stop altogether. I would stand on a chair and bang on the ceiling of the TV room, to no avail. It was as if someone up there was making a Walt Disney film about mischievous squirrels. I could imagine all their cute little faces and big guileless eyes, their bodies frozen in a dead stop and a look that said plainly, "It's her again with her broom handle, thinking she can stop us from having fun. Ha ha ha, he he he." Then off they'd go again, scampering back and forth.

That day, I had to go out, so in the end I just let them be – I didn't know what else to do about them.

Opening the back door, I passed through to the outside, carrying my umbrella because there was a light rain – goodness knows we needed it, so I had no complaint to make about that. It was what I saw that 'made my blood run cold', as they say. (Perhaps people don't say that any more. I say things sometimes that my mother used to say when I was a child.) Anyway, it wasn't so dreadful, what I saw, although it would have been if the cats had been lions and I had been the one in between them.

What I saw were the two cats, crouched, tails twitching and ready to spring, with a tiny mouse frozen between them on the grass. The poor mouse knew (I'm sure it was a she – so clever, as it turned out), she absolutely knew, that if she made the slightest movement, she'd have had it! That was another thing people used to say – 'You've had it, pal.' I don't speak like that and never did. I might have yelled, 'My god, look out!' It wouldn't have helped. The mouse had had it!

Transfixed, I found that, without realising it, I had lowered my unfurled umbrella to the ground so it became a sort of large bowl right there beside the fearful tableau. Then – oh joy! – in the blink of an eye, the clever little mouse leapt up and across – airborne – to land right inside the bowl. How did she know? She had no time to look or think about what do to.

And me – how could I have anticipated what she did?

But I played my part perfectly. The moment she landed safely, I did not hesitate. I picked up the umbrella with its tiny cargo, turned my back on the cats and walked calmly away to another part of the garden, where that resourceful mouse could at least have another chance at life. Ψ

Illustration: Eileen with umbrella at Lulworth House, Sydney, 2020, digitally transported to a garden in Havana, Cuba (background photo by Catherine Gray).

Fireflies

One summer, Miss Rita Fenshaw, a visitor from New York, was staying in a little house that looked out onto a wooded valley outside the town of Hinton in West Virginia.

The house had once been a schoolhouse for the children of the valley. It had only one room, and a wide wooden deck out front. If you stood on the deck you had a view of the whole valley and the mountain range behind it.

There were only a few houses in the valley. About 16 other people lived there, but Rita only rarely caught sight of them, as they walked past on the mountain road below the house.

In the daytime, the dogs of the nearest neighbour, Ray McCoy, could be seen and heard chasing other animals about. But each night, Ray kept them in at home with him.

No one used the land for farming – it was too steep – and there were no domesticated animals except for a few ducks and drakes that wandered about in Ray's yard.

So the valley was a peaceful one.

Rita was a painter. She liked the peace and quiet and was glad she didn't have too many people coming to see her. She didn't know the other people in the valley anyway and didn't encourage them to visit.

Her only companion was her cat. When she had first

got him, his name was Jesse. But she had been calling him Mr Puss for so long she thought it was about time she officially changed his name.

In truth, even as she painted her trees, her mountain ridges and the flow of the creek, or a human form walking along the road, she began to feel a little bit lonely. So did her cat.

The valley seemed so still and quiet. But at night, if she listened carefully, out of the silence would come the sounds of myriad invisible creatures. She would start to hear a long hum, and then, emerging through the hum, she could make out small clicks, pinpoint squeaks, moans, hiccups, long swishing sounds and faraway calls. The snapping of a twig could silence it all for a moment, and then it would resume, carried to her on the structure of the air.

She knew these sounds were real, not figments of her imagination, and she was excited. She listened searchingly, trying to discern the animal or insect from which the sounds came. But no; no creature appeared. She hadn't expected it to, really.

These were the sounds of life forms that were invisible to her. She wondered whether her cat could see or hear them. He was a bright cat, as close to her as any dog would be, but without all the tail-wagging and fuss with which dogs express their love.

One dark night, she was feeling her solitude keenly. As she sat communing with Mr Puss on her deck, the hum and the clicks and the swishes started up – the invisible creatures awakening to the glorious night. Then a new sound began to swell, as if a million tiny motors were revving up, until it all came to a sudden stop and a million fireflies took to the air, transforming the valley into a great wing of darkness studded with moving points of light. The stars opened up in the sky to meet the mountain tops.

Astounded, Rita yearned for someone or something to share her rapture. She looked down at her cat and, responding to her gaze, he looked up at her. His eyes seemed to say, "Isn't it marvellous, isn't it wonderful. We are in this together."

On such a night as this, Miss Rita Fenshaw, the artist, and Mr Puss, her magical cat, sat side by side, united in their connection to the great ommmm of the universe. **Ψ**

Illustration: Drawing by Eileen Kramer; also provides the background for 'The bees'.

The tiger

Renata was married to a man who didn't know how to make love. He was a scientist in search of an answer to the mystery of black holes in the sky. Most of his thinking went into that search, but that was really no excuse.

Renata was a fashion model. She believed a man should know how to please his wife, to give her the pleasure of love. Instead, as it turned out, Renata found herself giving all the pleasure, hoping all the while that Paul would learn from what she did for him.

He loved her, of course, and she loved him. She wasn't aware of the resentment building within her, until one day, Paul asked her if she would like to come with him to London, where he was taking part in a conference and other meetings for his work.

After thinking about this, Renata said that since her friends Jog and Lela had been asking her for some time to visit them in Mumbai, perhaps she would go to India instead.

Paul looked mildly surprised, but agreed that she should do that. So he went off to London and she bought two new summer dresses and flew to Mumbai.

Jog and Lela were at the airport to meet her and the three of them had a happy reunion. The women had gone to high school in Adelaide together so had known each other a very long time.

After spending a few days in the big city, with all it had to offer, Jog and Lela said they needed to drive to Panjim, in Goa. They were taking their cook with them, as he wished to visit his parents. "Cook grew up in Panjim," they said, "so he'll look after us."

Lela said they would have to pass through a jungle, and Jog said he'd take his gun to protect them should tigers or other wild animals threaten them. They didn't really expect that to happened because they'd been there before, but they thought it would excite Renata to feel she was in the India she had always dreamed of.

Renata was pleased. She had read a poem by William Blake that thrilled her. It began: "Tyger Tyger, burning bright/In the forests of the night". The prospect of passing through the jungle – the forests of the night – was irresistible. She could feel her spirit start to stir, to reach out beyond her body. But she didn't realise just how fascinating the trip would turn out to be.

They set off the next morning. Renata sat in the back with Lela, while cook, who fancied himself in charge of the expedition, sat next to Jog in the front.

The road was busy with cars and bicycles and trucks, and crowded with the usual kinds of travellers: old men with hoards of grandchildren, buffalos dragging carts or drays piled high with worldly goods; bossy men and self-effacing wives either riding or walking.

A lovely young woman in a sari on one of the over-loaded buffalo carts caught Renata's eye. It was the girl's stillness and natural grace that attracted her, perched as she was on what must have been an uncomfortable seat. Renata compared her unselfconscious poise with the artificially 'interesting' poses of western fashion models. The girl did not move, not once, while Renata, in the car, shifted about and changed her position often.

The whole scene – the buffalo, the wooden cart, the dignity of the girl – made Renata think of Paul, and how she had become enslaved, in a way, by always giving pleasure to him during their love-making. She wondered at this girl, who seemed so calm and self-possessed. Surely she would not give more to her lover than he gave to her. She would not experience the kind of resentment or frustration that Renata had felt building within her. Renata realised she no longer knew herself.

The traffic soon began to ease and the travellers were able to go on their way, leaving the buffalo cart behind.

The road went on. Sometimes they passed a palace or a temple; sometimes small villages; once a teacher on a mat under a tree, instructing another mat full of children; once, a man with a snake rising out of a basket to the sound of his flute or whatever the instrument was.

Later that afternoon, they reached the border of Goa, where they had to get their permits to travel on to Panjim. There was only one other person in the customs shed, a spacious building with a tin roof. He said he'd been waiting for over an hour for the officials to return a bottle they had taken away, for some reason, to be weighed.

Eventually, they were given the papers they needed but by then the afternoon had grown late and Jog was concerned about travelling through the jungle at night.

They set off, and as they came to the edge of the jungle, Jog's fear came to pass: the sun sank below the horizon. Cook warned them earnestly about the dangers ahead. On the right, he said, there was a sheer drop of hundreds of feet down to a snake-ridden valley, and on the left, the jungle was full of wild beasts.

Jog gripped the wheel, negotiating the curves of the road as cook urged him on: "To ze left, to ze right, to ze right, and to ze left…" Lela and Renata clung to each other.

It was very dark by now.

Suddenly, a pair of eyes shone brightly out of the darkness on the right side of the car. They were gone in a moment, but for Renata, they touched something deep within her. Sitting next to the door, she pushed the handle and jumped out. Before Jog could stop the car and run around to see what was happening, she was gone.

They searched for her as well as they could by the light of one small torch, but could find no trace. Jungle guides came but they too failed.

Where was Renata? Cook said she had been taken by the great spirit-tiger, or perhaps another spirit who stole people.

The fact was, after jumping out of the car, she had run straight ahead down a path that had miraculously opened up before her. At the far end of the path, she could see a light burning brightly − not a fire, but the bright radiance of the tiger. As she reached the end of the path and stopped, their eyes locked, and they looked deeply into each other. The tiger made no move towards her, his great body still.

Renata closed her eyes, feeling their spirits meet, then pass across, rippling from one to the other. When she looked again, she saw before her, not the tiger, but a man, handsome in a scholarly way, with intelligence in the lines of his face and tenderness in his gaze. It was no illusion: he was a man, but somehow he looked tiger-ish as well.

His look told her plainly that he was there for her, should she be there to take him, not as slave or master, but as two beings joined as one. She could not read any more from his eyes, except that he was for her.

She went with him without hesitation, even knowing that he had come from the world of the tiger.

His home was a hollow tree, comfortable, warm and smooth inside. There were no spiders and ants, but there was everything conducive to lovers moving freely about without being bitten or scratched. That was where she went to live with him, with no thought of her other life.

He taught her and she found out how nice it was to lie back, and let someone else give her pleasure for a change. Not always, but sometimes, so that they could share, each giving, each receiving.

Time was suspended. It was as though some strong hand had sculpted them into a single form. There was no long day spent apart, no separation between thoughts of love and those things that must be done by humans and animals alike.

Then the time came for her to go.

They had a goodbye talk. He said, "If they ask you how you lived while you were away, you can say a huge tree sheltered you, and you ate nuts and berries. Or coconuts. Sometimes bananas. Usually they say berries."

She said, "I don't know what I'm going to say to Paul. He knows I don't like berries very much."

He escorted her down the path, back to where she had jumped out of the car – how long ago? "Don't worry," he said. "Someone will come along soon and find you. They always do." And with that, he kissed her hand and left.

Meanwhile, in London, Paul and a forceful but nice woman were also making goodbye speeches to each other. She was a fellow scientist; perhaps there was something mysterious and tiger-ish about her too.

He said, "I don't know if I should say anything… I mean, about you."

She replied, "You needn't mention me. Just say you missed her, and have been thinking, and realised you should have followed her example when making love. Say you want to make up for it."

He said, "That's just what I will say. You really are a remarkable woman. I won't forget you."

Then she said, "Don't let her feel I've been teaching you. It must seem to come from you – from your own burning desire. Don't forget that."

"Goodbye," she said finally. "I'm glad you weren't silly enough to get yourself lost in a black hole."

"So am I," he said. Ψ

Illustration: 'Forest on the way to Goa', Eileen Kramer (tempera on tissue), painted from memory in London, c. 1960.

The crow

On the balcony of her room at the Taj Hotel in Mumbai, Paula Radford was about to have tea and a piece of scrumptious cake.

The Taj is not, as some people call it, the 'Taj Mahal', but just the 'Taj'. The Taj Mahal is quite a long way away. It was built by Shah Jahan as a memorial to his beloved wife Mumtaz Maha, reputed to be a clever, wise and beautiful woman. It is said that when the Shah called his minions to the palace to discuss affairs of state his wife would sit behind a curtain and listen. Afterwards she and the Shah would go over all that had been said and she would help him come to the final decision.

Paula, with teapot poised, pondered the romantic story of the Shah and his wife. She was sure he loved her not just for her beauty but because she was also clever and wise and he could talk to her. Whether this was true or not, she had no idea – after all, they were of the 17th century and she, Paula, was of the 20th. But she chose to believe it anyway.

Seated on her balcony, ready to pour out her cup of fragrant tea and lift to her sweetly open mouth her piece of cake, she felt beautiful herself. This was not just a lovely dream; it was true. She loved her beautiful face and was thankful for it. In a way, however, it kept her admirers at a distance. She'd never had a boyfriend or a lover. Of course, there was still time; she was only 22. One day the right man would enter her life. She believed that, so everything was all right.

All around the balcony, birds were flying and making their own love songs. The sound was a pleasant kind of burbling one. She had noticed it first thing that morning, when she was awakened for breakfast in bed. The sound was a delightful accompaniment to the scent of the rolls on her breakfast tray.

Paula hoped the birds, who were black, were ravens, not ordinary crows. Ravens would have been more romantic, and she wanted to feel romantic. But she couldn't distinguish one from the other. She wasn't a bird fancier; she was a dancer.

Thinking about the black birds reminded her of her own crow dance and the crow masks she had made for the two girls who did the dance. It was a gavotte. The masks had long pointed beaks and the costumes had wide wing-like sleeves, with the shapes of feathers along the edges. It had been an amusing dance, as the two crows bowed and opened their wings and met, parted and so on, until the end of the well known gavotte music.

Paula smiled as she remembered that the dances she loved most of all for herself were soft and expressive, mostly of love. She had never danced the strong or aggressive dances that suited her friend Olivia, and she didn't even leap, as Shona did. All she ever wanted was to feel herself dancing to the expressive music of tender emotions.

That might have been another thing that scared the men away. She tried to put such thoughts aside. She didn't want them to take charge!

The tea was flowing out of the spout of the teapot. Soon her cup would be lifted to her lips and she would drink. And also take a small bite of the cake. It was not a soft sponge cake but a firm pound cake with a faint perfume of almonds.

After the first sip of the tea, which really was just right, not too hot but not at all weak or just starting to lose its heat as some tea does, she chose the corner of the cake into which she would insert her silver cake fork.

Slowly, daintily, she would lift that corner to her lips and in one moment more would taste the rather sophisticated, she imagined, flavour of the almonds.

It was so good to be sitting on the balcony, with the gateway to India so close below and the heat making one feel languid in one's elegant new white summer dress – and the water of the bay so close, with the small boats waiting by the stone jetty to take one to the island of Elephanta; the beggars and the water sellers and the holy men, both Hindu and Moslem; and women in saris under the great arch – all so picturesque. Paula was in utter bliss.

Her hand holding its fork was coming closer to her lips, her mouth ready to receive the cake, when, as swiftly as the blink of an eye, a dark shape brushed her wrist. A black bird had passed between her hand and her lips, and flown away with her cake in his beak.

Paula was so startled that she uttered a loud cry, causing the young man next door to jump up from his own cup of tea and run to the low wall that separated their two balconies.

"What happened?" the young man cried. "Are you hurt? Those birds! Let me help."

Leaping quite easily over the dividing wall, he came to her side, and Paula, with a faint sigh — or was it a hiccup? — sank into his arms.

That was the beginning of a love affair that neither of them had expected. Without any time to be put off by her beauty and grace, he fell in love with her. And she with him.

All because of a cheeky crow that stole her piece of cake, on a balcony overlooking the gateway to India.

The young man's name, by the way, was Enrico and, with her help, he would one day become a famous singer. She herself would become a famous dancer, loved by all. Ψ

Illustration: Drawing by Eileen Kramer, 2020.

The horse

In the early days of Sydney, not so long after the invasion, people were sometimes lonely for what they called 'home', and performing artists from the 'old countries' always found grateful audiences when they toured around. One such company of 'dancing girls', as they were called, came to the colonies several times.

This was no great ballet company with expensive scenery and an orchestra. It was a small group of charming girls who had been trained not only to dance expressively but also to have good manners and to dress well. And they had to be strong enough to cope with the rigours of travel as well as the sometimes primitive facilities of the places where they performed.

Each girl had her own special talent: one could turn and twirl beautifully, another could leap gracefully, yet another was very good at expressing emotion. All could transform themselves through their dancing, and all looked perfectly radiant in whatever they did. The people loved them.

But there was one who seemed to have almost magical powers of transformation. As she danced, she would, before everyone's eyes, turn into a lovely white horse. She did this remarkable thing so slowly, so easily and so without hoop-la or showmanship, that audiences accepted it as natural. There were no cries of wonder or disbelief. She simply became a dancing horse that they loved.

This was Greta, and her dancing horse was so popular that Mr Crick, who handled their advance publicity, made a feature of it on their posters and leaflets.

Although the girls felt like one family, Greta's closest friend was Jean, a girl with long dark hair and sparkling eyes. Jean's special talent was noticing when things were going wrong and making them right. Her advice on everything from train timetables to hairstyles and boyfriends was always sensible. She was the closest thing they had to a road manager, and she often advised Greta not to do this or that.

As it happened, one evening after the performance, Mr Crick brought a man backstage to meet Madame Nevsky, the group's director, who had trained the girls from childhood. Mr Crick introduced the man as Mr Low Yen. Mr Low, he said, had been enchanted by Greta's performance and wanted to show her something that would in turn delight her.

"Yes," said Mr Low, bowing deeply to Madame. "This is the time of year when we must honour the mystery of the Horse."

Madame Nevsky, reassured by Mr Low's cultured manners and appreciation of Greta's talent, agreed that she could go with him, as long as Jean went along too. The girls looked pleased about that – they went everywhere together anyway – so they set off with Mr Low, in his carriage, to see whatever was going to delight them.

Sydney then was still only quite small, and they did not have to go very far. There were no electric lights on the streets, and there were few tall buildings, although the one they stopped in front of, which seemed to be some kind of Chinese temple, was fairly large. Jean and Greta knew what a temple looked like; they were studious girls and had learned about the world through Magic Lantern slides.

Following Mr Low inside, they passed through a handsomely decorated gateway into a wide courtyard with the temple rising up in the middle. On the far side of this courtyard was a beautiful white horse. He stood as still as a statue, so that the girls could not say whether he was alive or not.

Jean admired the animal, appreciating its beauty, but Greta was indeed delighted, just as Mr Low had said she would be. "Just wait," he said. "There is more delight to come."

He led the girls to a long wooden bench with the same carved design as the gate and politely took his leave, telling them he would come back for them soon. They sat and waited, not afraid, but interested in what might happen.

From where they sat, they could see a faint light coming from inside the temple, through double doors that did not quite meet. They could just make out a number of figures moving gracefully in the shadows. As the doors opened, the figures came slowly into the courtyard, seeming to transform themselves as they moved, from human to animal and back again, animal to human. Once they had gathered in the space in front of the temple, they formed a group that suggested they were about to dance.

The white horse had now taken the lead at the head of

the double line of figures. Was he a horse, or a dancer? His body seemed to glow, and his eyes radiated human intelligence. Greta clutched Jean's arm and looked at her, eyes wide with a sort of puzzled excitement.

"No, Greta," said Jean to her friend. "No."

The horse figure lifted his right front leg, holding it for a moment then extending it as though cutting sensuously through the air. The other figures then took up the dance, lifting and extending their legs as he had done. A moment ago, they had looked human; now, they were all beautiful horses. Jean thought of Greta's skill in transforming herself and knew this was the illusion of the dance.

But Greta said, "Oh! Is it really happening? It's magical."

She was already in love. She leaned back and looked at the moon, just visible now that a cloud had passed over it. She knew she was lost.

The dancers ended in human form. They smiled and bowed, and faded away into the shadows − all except the leader, who crossed the courtyard and stood before them, silvery in the moonlight.

"Your dance was very effective," said Jean. "I particularly admired the foot work."

"Thank you," he said, inclining his head towards Jean. But his eyes were locked with Greta's.

"Greta, we must go," Jean tried again. "Don't forget we have a show in Adelaide next week."

"You go," said Greta. "I may come later."

Jean knew at this point that she no longer had any power

over Greta. She kissed her friend, wished her well and went off to find Mr Low. "Oh dear," she thought. "What will I say to Madame?"

Back at the hotel she found Madame Nevsky in the lounge nursing a cup of cocoa. Madame raised her lorgnette and looked at Jean. "So, vere is our Greta, then?" she said.

"Oh Madame," said Jean. "I'm afraid I have to tell you: Greta is not coming back."

"I knew it," said Madame. "Ach! She has fallen in love."

Jean, ever practical, was thinking about how they would replace Greta's dance in the next performance. "We will need to change the advance publicity for Adelaide, Madame," she said. "We can just take the horse off the posters for now. I'll arrange it with Mr Crick."

"Thank you, my dear," said Madame. "It is these country tours; there is always some girl who does not come back."

She looked regretful, but inside, she was already thinking about creating a new dance for someone else. Who could it be?

"Eileen is coming along vell," she said. Ψ

Illustration: Detail of drawing by Eileen Kramer for her novel The Heliotropians, *Trafford Publishing, 2009.*

The tortoise

They say time does not exist out there in space. A strange thing, that. If there is no time, one cannot start a story with 'Once upon a time' and that would be a pity.

Anyway, once upon a time, and also more recently, there was an enchanted tortoise living in a small, enclosed space in the Botanic Gardens in Sydney, New South Wales. It had lived there, in measured time, since 1872. A sea captain had raided a tortoise community on the Galapagos Islands, stolen two grown animals and given one to the Queensland Botanic Gardens and one to the Gardens in Sydney. Who knows, he may have left young ones crying for their mothers, growing up with weird defects as a result. We'll never know that, really, so I'm sorry I even thought of such a thing.

The tortoise given to the Gardens in Sydney became enchanted when it noticed that time existed. Being deprived of its children or, on the other hand, its mother, had an interesting effect on its mind: it thought it knew how to speak, and if that's not enchanted, I don't know what is.

In the course of its long, long life, it talked to many visitors to the Gardens, telling them many things about how, for instance, the quaint cottage close to its enclosure got to be built, and who lived there, as time passed, as it must, and who was good at scratching the backs of heads, and who was silly enough to turn tortoises upside down to find out what they were – man or not man – and what kind of food it liked and whether it always went slowly or whether it ran when it saw the postman coming – ran to find out whether there was a letter for it.

Well, not very many people passed that way, and what with no letters coming, and no other tortoises turning up from the Galapagos, it stands to reason the tortoise was sometimes lonely.

It would sometimes sing to itself, "Pale hands I loved beside the Shalimar…" It remembered this song from way back. A burly-looking man from a ship – a lugger, perhaps – would come ashore and say in a loud voice, "What you need is a good rousing song about God, so come on now, all together," and so all the tortoises sang the only song they knew, about the person's hands beside the Shalimar. The man would turn a kind of purple and wack a few of them, then stalk off muttering "Heathens, that's what they are."

Let us leave the tortoise for the moment, in its time-less world singing a ballad of olden days about someone's hands, and change the scene – to a place where time passed in ordinary fashion, and where there was a young wom-an whose name was Lady Alice Incubator, although her friends sometimes called her 'Roly Poly' behind her back.

On this particular day, a fine and sunny one, Lady Alice stepped down from the building where she lived, with the intention of going for a walk. Not a very original idea, it must be said, but it suited her. She took twenty-five paces across the street and at a slightly later point in time entered the Botanic Gardens by the imposing side entrance – the Rose Gate.

Passing through the rose garden, whose perfume made her swoon with exotic pleasure, she crossed the lawn and from there passed along many shaded laneways, passages and avenues, and in and out of arbours full of queer smells, until she came to a small grassy area covered with strange leaves and branches and bits of yellow rock on the ground. Her way was blocked by a sort of wall, made of stone, with a young man's face protruding over the top.

"Damn – and I wanted to be alone!" the young man said to himself.

But Alice had looked up and seen him so he came down and joined her.

"Don't I know thee, O maiden?" he said politely.

"Of course you do, silly," she replied. "We meet almost every day in the coffee shop where I live."

"I didn't know you lived in the coffee shop," he said, and they sat down on the soft grass together.

Soon, Lady Alice realised it was unwise to sit in this secluded spot with a young man she only knew from the coffee shop. Lord Incubator might get the wrong idea. So she suggested to the young man, whose name turned out to be Sir Thomas Tallyrand, that they go for a walk.

"I want to show you something," she said.

Eventually, they came upon the fenced-off place where

the tortoise lived. "This is Thomas the Tortoise," said Alice.

The tortoise raised its head, very slowly — yes, we are back with the enchanted tortoise, disturbed from its timeless reverie.

"I have to tell you one thing," it said. "My name is not Thomas, and I'm not a boy or a man. I am a woman and proud of it."

"Good heavens," exclaimed the real Thomas. "That's two things actually! But I'm so sorry, of course. You're a delightfully lovely woman too."

"I too am sorry," said Lady Alice, frowning. "No woman likes being called a man. You have every right to be angry."

"I'm not. I just want everything clear and open," said the tortoise.

At that, the door of an old-fashioned cottage nearby opened and a lady with a little boy came out.

"Oh, I see you have met mademoiselle," she said, and pointed to the tortoise, who blushed.

"She thinks I'm French," said not-Thomas, "But I'm not. It's just that I have that way about me."

The tortoise then told them the whole story of how the sea captain had purloined her friend, the Queensland tortoise, and herself, on the Galapagos Islands, and brought them to Australia.

"That is God's truth," she added, and so Lady Alice and Sir Thomas believed her.

The little boy, whose name was Eveready Roger, piped up and said, "Yes, and she's mine, so don't start thinking you can take her away anywhere."

"Of course not, most certainly not, wouldn't dream of it," said Lady Alice, "Only maybe across the road to my place. That's not far is it, Sir Thomas?"

"Why are they talking so funny?" Eveready asked his mother.

The mother, whose name we do not know, explained away her son's rudeness. "He always says that. Please don't hold it against him, will you, Lady Et-cetera and Sir What's-your-name."

Lady Alice and Sir Thomas shook their heads, not wanting to embarrass the boy or his mother by introducing themselves properly.

"What about *my* name?" the tortoise cried. "Don't I get a proper name? After all, I can talk. Could I be Lady Roundtop?"

"Now, mademoiselle, you know we think you're lovely. A name is only a name and most people hate being called silly names," said Eveready's mother.

She turned to Sir Thomas and Lady Alice with a false smile and bid them good evening.

At home that night Lady Alice told her husband all about it. She was mortified. "What should we do?"

Lord Incubator merely drawled, "Don't take on so, my treasure. After all, look at it like this." He stood up as if to make a speech and what he actually said was, "A tortoise is a tortoise is a tortoise, my dear. Worse things could have been brought here from the Galapagos, so don't you fret."

She gazed at him in wonder. "But darling, when we met and began to love each other I never knew you could be so clever."

"Oh yes you did, you wicked lamb," was all he replied, and no truer word was ever spoken.

Except that none of this could have ever happened if the sea captain had purloined a dugong or a sea lion instead of Lady Roundtop, the enchanted tortoise.

That's the truth. Ψ

Illustration: Drawing by Eileen Kramer, 2018.

95

The rat

Once there was a dancer named Katya Kotova. Her real name was Clare Wellington but people had told her she could more easily get jobs as a dancer if she was Russian. She did once have a small part in *The Nutcracker*, but fame never really came her way.

This is a story about how Katya or Clare did something one day that filled her with remorse for the rest of her life. It happened on the very day she was to have an audition.

She was living in a room in someone else's apartment – back in the 1940s when you could still rent single rooms on Sydney's elegant Macquarie Street. And on that fateful moring, she had a song going round in her head – a popular song, nothing classical or Russian. She liked it. So she was singing to herself as she entered the bathroom.

You made me love you…

And then she saw it: a rat, a fairly large rat, poised on the windowsill above the washbasin. Acting instinctively, she took three paces through the room and with a single balletic sweep of her arm, knocked the rat right out of the window.

I didn't wanna do it, I didn't wanna do it…

The rat, floating earthwards, wailed, "The hell you didn't!" It landed with a thud on the striped canvas awning over the footpath café (the 'potted Dog, formerly the

Spotted Dog but now bereft of its 'S'). Then, scrabbling madly, it slipped over the edge and landed nose-first in a young man's cappuccino.

Upstairs in the bathroom, Clare or Katya or whatever she called herself, was beside herself with shock.

> *You made me do it*
> *And all the time you knew it*
> *I guess you always knew it…*

The rat meanwhile was trying clumsily to extract itself from the remains of the cappuccino. Chocolate and white froth dripped from its ears and whiskers.

The young man who had been about to take his first sip of the ill-fated coffee jumped to his feet in horror, knocking into an adjacent table where a woman was sitting with a big bag on her lap waiting for a taxi.

The bag was full of medicines – six different kinds of pills – from the chemist next to the 'potted Dog and they all went flying. A passing youth stopped to help, but as he bent over to pick them up he was bumped on his behind and went flying too.

Three girls at a nearby table leapt onto their chairs, screaming and checking their legs to make sure the rat hadn't climbed up under their skirts.

The lady with the pills almost fainted as the wind blew her hat off, and the young man who had lost his cappuccino rushed to her aid. But the rat, by now utterly discombobulated, ran up one of the man's trouser legs, causing him to jump about frantically in fear for his most sacred parts. He might have been doing a version of de Falla's 'Ritual Fire Dance' – although maybe not, as this was a style of dance no longer performed.

Whatever, the young man's balletic actions scared the rat out of his trouser leg and it slipped unnoticed into a nearby wicker basket, whose owner had carefully packed it full of art materials that morning, intending to spend the day in the Art Gallery copying a Tom Roberts portrait called 'Eileen'.

Upstairs, Clare/Katya, had retreated to her flatmate's couch, overcome by remorse.

You made me happy, sometimes you made me glad
But there were times, you made me feel so bad…

The three girls on the chairs had by now stopped scream- ing. They hastily climbed down, paid for their coffees and ran down the street, shouting to passers-by, "Don't go to the 'potted Dog; there's a rat… a rat!"

"Vot! Vot! You call me a rat? For zis I come to Austra- lia?" cried an elegantly dressed old man, shaking his stick at the girls.

The waiter finally came out to find out what was going on. He begged everyone to control themselves, denying absolutely that they ever had rats in the 'potted Dog. Dis- tressed, he tripped over the wicker basket containing the fugitive rat and banged into an elderly gentleman standing on the kerb, knocking him into the path of a delivery truck.

Only the swift action of the driver saved the man from being run over. The driver, in a state of shock, got angry and accused the waiter of pushing the old man on purpose.

Eventually the artist decided she'd had enough of all the commotion, so she picked it up her basket and walked over to the Art Gallery, where, instead of doing any painting, she devoted herself to quiet contemplation of the 'Queen of Sheba visiting King Solomon'. This was probably just as well, because unbeknownst to her, the rat was still in her basket, waiting patiently between a tube of blue paint and a box of charcoal for the sounds of the day to die away.

Back in Macquarie Street, Clare had forgotten she was supposed to be Russian and was trying to explain to her flatmate what had happened. "I'm not a cruel person," she said. "But a rat in the bathroom – really!"

"In Phillip Street, perhaps, but never in Macquarie Street," agreed the flatmate, a zoology student called Winnie. "Rats are not so nice. Give me a wombat, or a duck-billed platypus any day."

Clare sighed. She still felt bad about what she'd done.

"Well, I'm leaving now; make sure you lock up," said Winnie.

"Yes," said Clare, although by now she had given up on her audition. She thought she might just stay home instead.

> *Gimme, gimme, gimme, gimme what I cry for*
> *I've got the brand of kisses that you'd die for*
> *You made me love you...*

"All I wanted was a drink of water," said the rat, from inside the wicker basket in the Gallery.

Eventually it made its way back to the Sydney Showground, where it re-joined the circus it had run away from.

Clare went to Moscow after all, where she spoke Australian and taught people to sing and dance to tunes like "…once a jolly swagman camped by a billabong…" and "the dog sat on the tuckerbox five miles from Gundagai".

But she always felt sorry about the rat. Ѱ

Illustration: Domestic rat, Arco Christine / Getty Images.

Elephants

One day I wondered: what if life was like *Star Trek*? What if elephants had been first on the moon and taken control of the world?

They look so gentle and kind. Of course, if pushed they could be vengeful, but who wouldn't, if pushed. Mostly they are good, have great memories and look after each other, it is said. And they're not as stiff and ungainly as you might think. Their legs are flexible. Not that this would be relevant to managing the world and straightening out all its problems.

Would they be as great at being parliamentarians as they are supposed to be at living in herds in Africa or India or anywhere else they might be?

In animal videos they do many things.

A baby elephant looks so reasonable and clever riding on a child's trolley (or whatever it is) while two boys or dogs pull her along, that one feels sure she would grow up to be a wonderful parliamentarian.

A baby elephant walking along on the bank of a river, chasing a butterfly with his trunk, looks so charming that most people would vote for him when he grew up – assuming he stayed just as sweet and charming.

Would adult elephants be as reasonable and patient and wise in parliament as they look to be on an elephant walk?

So what if they push trees over with their superior

strength; they would not destroy all of the trees in the jungles of the world.

They're faithful too, to their friends. One imagines they would carry out what they promised to do.

I'm all for elephants.

Giraffes are reasonable animals too. Their legs look skinny but I wouldn't like to be kicked by one of them. Giraffes could be the media men and women, finding things out and writing about them, attending any meetings, listening to everyone, with their long necks helping them find out secrets.

A zebra could be the speaker of the house. Why? Because she has all those stripes. That's why.

And there could be kangaroos, as clerks, with files in their pouches.

And so on. There would be jobs for all the grass-eating animals. No lions or tigers. All those good animals wouldn't need anyone to keep order. Still, let's be a little bit suspicious and have a lion or two just in case.

Perhaps there'd also be a very long python that crossed the floor.

How does *Star Trek* come into this?

You remember the excellent Starship Enterprise and its crew, don't you? Captain Kirk, Bones, Mr Spock, and later the robot that had human feelings. All fantasy, with strange characters living on fantastic planets.

Those fantasies usually worked well, so why shouldn't this one?

Vote for the Elephants.

If you never saw the early *Star Trek* series, try to track them down. Ψ

Illustration: Drawing by Eileen Kramer, 2020.

"Sometimes you have a bunch of images
that seem unconnected. If you were a knitter,
you might knit them, with the magic of
numbers, into an exotic sweater or shawl.
If you were a writer or a dancer,
you might weave them into a story."

Part 2:
Just people

The tower

Elizabeth saw her life as an architectural composition, a kind of tower with new spaces added day by day, year by year – rooms, hallways, verandas, cupboards, pieces of furniture, and whole new storeys.

When she was seven years old, something happened that she later believed set the pattern for this complicated edifice.

She had been sitting close to two older girls who were talking to each other. They noticed her and one said to the other, "Isn't she pretty!" The other girl agreed; then the two, so much older than Elizabeth, gazed at her for a few moments before going on with their conversation.

Elizabeth stayed close to these girls for many days after, hoping to hear them say it again, or at least look at her again, and smile at her. They didn't do this. On the contrary, once they noticed her hanging around, they began to regard her as a nuisance.

As time passed and Elizabeth felt her life-tower begin to take form, she thought far too often of what the two girls had said.

She asked her mother, "Mummy, am I pretty?"

"Yes, my darling," her mother said. "You're the most pretty little girl I know." But not wanting Elizabeth to become overly concerned with her appearance, she added, "Don't think about that too much though. Learn your lessons – that will help you a lot more in life."

That last bit didn't please Elizabeth very much, and she didn't believe her mother really thought she was pretty. Learning her lessons was all very well − she did enjoy thinking about things − but none of it mattered very much if you weren't pretty.

In her teenage years she came home from high school one day and almost smothered herself with her mother's big powder puff. Face powder was the thing at that time. Red lipstick too. She looked, well, not pretty to be sure − more like a clown.

Elizabeth longed to be like Greta Garbo, and say, in a husky voice, "I just want to be alone." Greta Garbo wasn't actually pretty, but she had a wonderful face.

Elizabeth herself was alone in a way. She didn't let anyone know how she felt − how she still longed to hear someone say, "Isn't she pretty!" Hers wasn't a bad face to own up to, but she wanted too much; she wanted it to be perfect.

Her tower grew, adding more rooms with memories living in them. Elizabeth dropped in now and then to the room on the ground floor where the two schoolgirls lived, but they never again said what they had said.

In New York she went to the Martha Graham School of Dance. Martha herself didn't have a pretty face, only a striking bone structure. She said, "We don't want any geniuses here, and don't use the word 'pretty'. Just learn your craft; that is all I ask of you."

Elizabeth learned her craft, and while she was in Manhattan she also attended Zen Buddhist meditation sessions. So on the fifth floor of her life-tower there were now two big rooms, one for learning her craft, and the other for meditating and getting rid of the self – or trying to.

She went to Paris and became an artist's model to earn some money. There she added another room. It could have had pretty-girl memories dancing about, if it hadn't been for the self that made Elizabeth long for the pretty face. So it had mirrors that you could look into in search of Pretty.

Then the Beatles came along. They had a song that said, 'Will you still love me when I'm sixty four', or was it 'a hundred and four'. That didn't matter yet, for she was nowhere near sixty let alone a hundred and four. But she would be one day; that room was up there in the air, waiting.

Lovers came and went, but none of them said it. She wondered why – why didn't one, at least, say, "Elizabeth, you look so pretty in that dress." She couldn't love a man who couldn't feel it, even if he couldn't see it.

Back in London, there were pretty girls with pink and white complexions, but Elizabeth wasn't one of them. She'd been in the south of France getting sunbrown. She had managed to get tanned all over. She gave a dance performance on the stage of the Australia House concert hall.

In Paris, she continued to pose for artists. She learned how to project – what? The pose, or the meaning, or the inspiration, or something, that was in the room, with rest periods on the veranda provided just for her.

Time passed. The Beatles song kept running through

her head. Back and forth she went from London to Paris, waiting for someone to say she was pretty. Yes, she made a name for herself, but looking into the mirror she had her doubts even though she tried hard. "I really could be called pretty," she said. "Or maybe good-looking."

Still no one said it.

Then one day she went somewhere with a friend and found herself sitting on a couch next to a man who looked at her in quite a different way. She felt like she'd known him forever. Before she could say anything, she felt a strong hand pressing her upper body toward him, and two lips against hers, murmuring, "I love you; you're so beautiful."

"Not pretty?" she managed to say. They both spoke in a muffled way, being pressed so closely together. When she was released from the strong hand on her back, she took a deep breath and said, "Too late, too late. I was just about to say, too late, because I'll soon be a hundred and five. Will you still love me, when I'm a hundred and five? Will you find me pretty?"

"Oh my darling, how can you ask me that! I think you're the most beautiful, the prettiest, woman in the world!"

This moment of course went straight into the loveliest room in the great tower of Elizabeth's life. And they lived as happily as could be in that room without her ever having to look in the mirror to make sure his words were true. Ψ

Angels

In the Bible story of Cain and Abel, Cain kills his brother Abel, who is a herder of sheep. Cain is a tiller of the soil. Maybe he wanted Abel's share of the land, but that shouldn't have been enough to make him kill his own brother.

Madame Bodenwieser, in her dance drama based on this story, gave Cain motivations of jealousy, hatred, greed and fear. Her choreography plan had Shona, as Cain, leaping wildly into the air after the murder, in exaltation. Shona also had to lean over Abel's body in fear that he may not really be dead. When she performed this, Shona would gently pick up Abel's arm then let it go. The arm would fall back lifelessly, and all of the audience, and those of us waiting in the wings, would feel Cain's horror and fascination and fear. Shona did it so well.

Madame herself was to take the role of the mother who finds Abel's body at the end, with us new girls as angels looking down on them. This filled us with awe: Madame had been our teacher for several years, and we had never even thought of her dancing, let alone being in the same scene with her.

When the company started work on this dance drama, Madame said the angels would not be needed until she started rehearsals for the last scene. So I had some free time, and when a girl I knew, Joan Dignam, asked me and

Mary Douglas, another angel, to take jobs as artists in a toy factory, we said yes. Mary wasn't really an artist but my friend said it would be very easy for her.

We discovered just how easy on the first day.

The factory consisted of two rooms in a house on lower George Street, near Circular Quay. The young man who owned the business made very small animals in a mould. That was step one. Then, at step two, an elderly man who also worked for him placed the animals carefully in rows on a tray and brought them up to a room on the next floor, to the so-called Art Department – me, Mary and Joan – where we would paint them, delicately applying spots to the cheetahs and giraffes and stripes to the zebras and tigers. I called Joan 'the boss', since she had found us the job. I was 'the staff', and Mary was 'the girl' because she was the youngest. Mary had to make the morning tea at eleven o'clock – although as an angel-to-be, she didn't think that was right.

The elderly man, Mr Hill, came to our room several times a day with his tray full of giraffes and cheetahs and zebras and tigers. He would say conscientiously every time, "Now girls, please remember to paint the eyes on the giraffes."

And every day, by late morning, we would find ourselves responding to his entrance with helpless giggles or shrieks of laughter. This hurt his feelings of course. What we didn't realise though, was that by then we were high as kites from all the paint fumes – so it wasn't our fault.

Anyway, the Art Department didn't stay together very long. The exodus started with Joan. One day at about 12 o'clock, a handsome young man appeared in the doorway. Joan looked up and froze, gazing at him with her paintbrush suspended in the air. Then, as if in a trance, she rose from her seat, scattering brushes and paints, pushed back her chair, walked to the doorway and went – without her good shoes, which she left under the table. We didn't see her again for a week.

A few days after that, we had a call from Evelyn (Abel), who said we should come immediately to the Conservatorium of Music, where rehearsals were about to start for the angel scene.

To our discredit, we didn't even explain to Mr Hill why we were leaving in a hurry. I imagine him with his tray of giraffes and zebras, standing in the doorway of an empty Art Department. It was cruel of us – to him, as well as to the young man trying to make a business for himself. I was a bit sad about it afterwards.

But at that moment, as Mary and I made our way across from George Street to the Con, all we could think about was our upcoming role as angels.

We would be wonderful. All we had to do was wait until the stage lights went off, climb onto a wooden tower-like structure making sure our fluttering chiffon wings didn't get caught, and take our beautiful poses. Below us, Madame herself stood with outstretched arms, expressing in her true central European modern dance style, the message of the drama – that the spirit of the victims of oppression would live on and be remembered.

Well, that was how Madame had choreographed it, but it almost didn't turn out that way.

Madame had lately made the acquaintance of an actress whom she greatly admired. She saw, or imagined she saw, in this person a highly dramatic quality and spiritual power. So she asked her to play the very top angel – standing at the apex of the wooden tower.

On the night of the dress rehearsal, which quite a lot of people had come along to see, this great actress of Madame's arrived at the very last minute. Not only was she decked out in sequins, but she had also been drinking. There was no time to spare. She knew what she had to do. Madame couldn't stop her. She got herself up to the top of the tower, and stood there swaying from side to side with a foolish smile on her face, all through Madame's arm-raising hope-for-mankind dance.

Of course, on the night of the actual performance, it had to be one of us new girls who took that place at the top of all the angels, and to my great joy, it was me. Ψ

Illustration: Shona Dunlop as Cain for the Bodenwieser Ballet production Cain and Abel, *performed in the Conservatorium of Music's Verbrugghen Hall in 1940. Photograph by Margaret Michaelis, courtesy of the Cuckson-Bodenwieser Archive.*

The man

Not so long ago and not so far away, there was a building with a doorway into a corridor that led nowhere.

When Sue first came across this mysterious doorway, it was empty. But then she blinked and a tall handsome man was standing there. He looked like the kind of man who was capable of taking life seriously without going off the deep end – cool and well able to deal with things.

The doorway puzzled her. There was no door attached, and it was slightly askew, so that both it and the man seemed to be leaning toward the west. After a few moments of looking she found she rather liked it.

Thinking something was expected of her, Sue took a step forward, but suddenly the man was no longer there.

That was when she noticed the corridor beyond the doorway. Although brightly lit, it didn't lead to anything. It simply stopped. This was a mystery indeed. There was no sign of the man.

She saw him again on several occasions after that. Once, she saw him on the gangplank of the Manly ferry. She was waiting for another ferry but forsook it so she could hurry over to the Manly side of the wharf. There, the same strange thing happened. As she went to step onto the gangplank she saw that, like the mysterious corridor, it didn't go anywhere – the bright sunlight must have been creating an illusion, she told herself. The man had disappeared too. She was just thankful she'd stopped herself in time, or else she'd have been floating about with a mouthful of dirty Circular Quay water.

The third time was outside her own house. She was standing waiting to cross the road when a group of bikies stopped at the lights. And there he was in the lead, a heroic figure all in white on a bike with silver trim. She spoke to him directly, without thinking. "You look very nice," she said.

He looked back at her and said with the same feeling, "So do you."

She knew this was probably true, for she was also all in white, wearing a long, high-waisted dress, with her hair hanging down over one shoulder, and a wicker basket over her arm. It was a romantic moment, the kind one never forgets.

The lights changed. All the bikies on their bikes surged forward with a roar, and simply disappeared, along with the road and her front gate.

She blinked several times, and suddenly – never mind the Manly ferry, never mind the bikies – there she was again at the mysterious doorway, and there he was standing before her.

This time Sue noticed something she hadn't seen before: a low narrow step. Placing one foot in front of the other, she took the three paces necessary, mounted that one step, and – lo and behold – for the first time, the very first out of all the times she had seen him, she felt his warmth.

Without hesitation, without an unnecessary word, his arms came around her, held her close, as did hers, in the same way, around him. Ψ

Illustration: Photograph by Sue Healey in James Turrell's Skyspace installation 'Within Without', National Gallery of Australia, Canberra.

2I's
COFFEE BAR

The artist's model

Four girls who lived together in an old terrace house in London were having breakfast one morning when the phone rang. Mary Wetherton, closest to the phone, answered it. She seemed doubtful at first but then looked at Lucy Bower and said, "It's a man. He wants to speak to the artist's model. It'll be for you, Lucy."

The other two girls, Faith Dunlop and Greta Taber, stopped buttering toast and listened as Lucy took the phone.

They were an unlikely group to be living together but were quite fond of each other. One was a law student, one was into science and studying to be a nurse and one had just started work as a primary school teacher. Only Lucy had no such aspirations. She was happy earning a living as an artist's model, a job that on the surface didn't seem to need any special skill. This wasn't quite true, however, for she needed to be able to create and hold a pose, giving part of herself in order to project the required image for those who sat before her striving to capture it.

The man said he was calling from Brighton. "I've seen you on the model's stand, and that's what I'm calling about."

He went on to explain that he'd been working for an artist in Bristol who was about to start on a large subject – the 'Four Seasons'.

"Oh," thought Lucy, "that same old subject." But she was happy to hear what he had to say. He gave his name: Basil Roper, an artist's model, like herself.

During a short pause during which Basil seemed to be shuffling some papers, Lucy mouthed the words, "Another artist's model," to her roommates.

"The painter I've been working for," Basil said, now back from his papers, "has asked me to find a female model who can commit herself to a couple of months' work. He has a very big house with his own studio and lots of rooms, so he could provide accommodation. You wouldn't have to do any other work. He also has a cook–housekeeper who would look after us."

Before Lucy could say anything or ask about payment, he went on, "He pays well. As matter of fact he's already given me money to pay you something in advance, and he wants me to take you out to dinner somewhere in London so that we can make each other's acquaintance. You would be the figure of 'spring'; I'm 'summer'. When he needs 'autumn' and 'winter' he'll ask me to find someone else. Are you interested?"

Lucy thought for a moment. She was not heavily booked and anyway, she could cancel the bookings she had. She liked the idea of going to Bristol and staying in a house where there was a housekeeper. She didn't even need to discuss it with her roommates. "Yes," she said. "I'll be glad to do it."

They decided there and then to meet for dinner the next

evening, which would be Saturday. Basil said he would give her the advance share of the money as soon as they met.

Lucy's roommates were excited for her and said Basil sounded like fun. The meeting was to be in a hotel somewhere in Piccadilly. "It's a large public lounge," he had said. "Take a taxi and wear something red so I'll know you." He giggled and added, "I've seen you, but never in your clothes." She said she'd wear a red carnation.

When she entered the lounge that Saturday evening, with the carnation duly pinned to her dress, she was almost overwhelmed by the cacophony of voices and the sight of so many young people laughing and talking with each other in the room.

She found a small table and sat down quickly before anyone else could take it, putting her bag on the other seat to let people see it was reserved. Within five minutes Basil turned up and she was glad to see he was fairly young and good-looking. He was friendly too, but a little bit business-like, she thought, as if he had just pulled off an important deal.

Before they went into the hotel's big dining room. Basil put a briefcase he was carrying onto the table. From it he produced an envelope, opened it and took out some bank notes.

"Here is the money," he said. "He wanted to be sure I would give it to you." Basil selected five twenty-pound notes and gave them to her. "The rest is for our dinner, and for me," he said.

She took the money without counting it, and as she leaned forward, her glance fell on a sheet of paper in the open briefcase, and a name and address written at the top of the page. It was not an extraordinary name, and there was no reason why she should take notice of it. In fact she hardly realised she had done so.

His transaction concluded, Basil suggested that since it was so noisy in the hotel, they should go somewhere else to dine. So they left together and he took her to a good small restaurant where they enjoyed their dinner. They talked a lot and he told her some quite amazing stories. She couldn't help thinking about how they would sound when she told her roommates about them later.

After dinner he said, "It's not over yet." She followed him through narrow streets, until they stopped before a three-storey terrace house somewhere in a darker part of Piccadilly. Leading her up the five steps to the entrance, he pressed the bell, and after a while, someone came to open the door — a burly man who looked as if he had the strength to throw anyone out if he had to.

He won't need to throw us out, Lucy thought to herself. She wasn't at all afraid, with Basil by her side.

When they entered the lobby, Basil spoke to another young man behind the counter of a small cloak room — not much more than a wall with shelves, and hooks for coats. Basil gave him the briefcase, which was then placed on the top shelf. She could see part of it poking out, and hoped it would be all right.

After a little friendly banter with the cloak room boy and some unexpectedly high-pitched laughter from the depths of the burly man who had let them in, Basil and Lucy were led to a door.

It was at this point that a sudden sense of weirdness overcame Lucy. And she only then remembered something Basil had said as they had walked through the dark narrow streets – something that she, with two years of proper experience as an artist's model, couldn't quite believe. He had said that one day, when he was posing at one of the London art schools, the head of the school had come into the studio and ordered Basil to come down from the model's stand and follow him: he was needed in another life drawing class. "He didn't even give me time to get my robe, so I had to walk stark naked along two corridors," Basil had said with a sort of shudder.

Lucy had dismissed this at the time as something that couldn't have happened: a model would never walk along the corridor stark naked.

But it came back to her now, and suddenly, the burly man, the cloak room boy, the narrow streets – the whole setup, in fact, and Basil in particular – felt weird to her.

Meanwhile, the burly man knocked on the door, still chuckling, and it was opened to allow them to step through into – what? A miniature theatre with about ten rows of seats, and a man in a towel sitting on a chair in the middle of a lighted stage.

There was just time for Basil and Lucy to take their seats

near the doorway, before an even brighter light flooded the stage, and six pert-looking naked girls, pink flesh gleaming through sheer plastic raincoats, ran onto the stage. They surrounded the seated man, jiggling about and tormenting him until at last they led him, clad only in his gym towel, off stage to whatever fate awaited him.

Lucy wasn't impressed. Once she was able to take it all in, she felt scornful, thinking it was very childish – not at all wicked, or even pornographic. She maintained this superior attitude throughout the next three scenes, until Basil suddenly got up from his seat, without a word, and left her, returning about five minutes later. He did this four times during the show, but after the fourth time, he didn't come back at all.

When the show was over, the house lights were turned on and the audience started filing up the aisle. She realised she was the only woman there. But the men hardly noticed her in their haste to get out the door and home to their wives.

Her concern was for Basil. What could have happened to him? She made a bit of a fuss, questioned the burly man, and tried to mount some stairs that led to an upper floor. She was about to turn away when she looked up and saw the briefcase, still protruding a little on the shelf behind the cloak room boy.

"That's his briefcase!" she cried dramatically.

"So it is," said their former pal, the burly man. He chuckled again, which struck her this time as highly inappropriate.

"Well," she asked, "What has happened to him?" Would he have gone away and left the case with all that money in it? She was glad she had been given her share already, although that wasn't the point right now. She continued to make a fuss, worried that Basil could be lying drunk or drugged in one of the upstairs rooms.

"You can take the briefcase if you like," said the young man behind the cloak room counter. "We don't want it."

Where would she take it? She calmed down, and wrote down the club's telephone number so she could call tomorrow to find out whether Basil had come back for his case.

She phoned her roommates to tell them all about it, but they couldn't make sense of what she was saying, so she hung up and called a taxi instead. She felt like the 'doll' from a Raymond Chandler mystery. Of course, by the time she got home, the girls were all agog! They wanted to know everything.

She called the club the next day, Sunday, but there was no answer. She called again on Monday, and they said there was no sign of Basil. She wanted to say, "Did you look in the upstairs rooms?"

On Tuesday she remembered the name and address she had seen in Basil's briefcase: Bob Collins, General Store, Putney. How strange that she should remember this, when she normally never, just never, remembered such things.

She looked up the number in the phone book (this was a time well before the internet) and dialled. A woman answered and when Lucy started to explain what she wanted, the woman called out to someone in another room. "Bob, I think it's for you."

There was a pause, then a man came on the line and Lucy tried to tell him the story. At last he seemed to understand and got quite excited.

"Do I know him? I'll say I do!" he said. "He's my son, and he ran away last week with all the money in my cash register!" Then he added, as if he really was a nice man, "If you've had anything to do with him, miss, I'm sorry for you. If you do hear from him, you'd better tell him that he's burned his bridges here, and he shouldn't bother coming home."

Lucy thanked him and hung up, none the wiser really.

But that wasn't quite the end of the story. One morning a few weeks later, Lucy was fulfilling a modelling engagement – which thank goodness she hadn't cancelled – at the Heatherley art school. As she stood on the model's stand, naked, like a queen, she saw the head of school enter the studio, showing someone around his wonderful facility. With a gracious gesture of his hand he indicated the students at work and the model on the stand. He looked proud.

Lucy lowered her eyes modestly, and as she did so she noticed the well-shod feet of the important visitor. She looked slowly up until she came to the visitor's face. Their eyes met.

Of course it was Basil, this time posing as the American head of the Students' Art League in New York!

Despite her surprise, Lucy controlled herself and held

her pose. Her duty was to inspire the young students seated before her with drawing pads and pens or charcoal, their gaze intently focused on her form.

But the head of school was stricken with concern when his important visitor had a sudden attack of something terrible and had to leave the room immediately.

"What next for Basil?" wondered Lucy, with a secret smile. She had to admit she was slightly relieved to know he had not perished in the upstairs room of a seedy club in Piccadilly. Ψ

Illustration: Eileen as life model, and photograph of the 2 I's Coffee Bar, Soho, 1959.

Kïsses

Arden Street ran from the Randwick cemetery, past our house, to Coogee Beach and then all the way to Bronte. The Coogee Life Savers clubrooms were right on the beach, at the southern end.

My friend Betty and I usually went to the dances held at the Life Savers every Saturday evening, and it was there that Betty's future life was formed.

We spent Saturday afternoons getting ready. We washed our hair, put egg white on our faces and walked about taking care not to get excited and spoil the effect of the egg, which would have dried and turned into a stiff mask.

Our mothers always left us alone for the whole afternoon – Betty and her mother Ann lived with me and my mother Hilda – so we had the breakfast room to ourselves, along with my sewing machine should we want to finish a dress to wear to the dance. We didn't make a new dress every Saturday of course, but we often had some other sewing to do.

At the clubhouse we paid our money and settled ourselves on the far side of the hall, facing the entrance doorway. From where we were standing, waiting for seats to be vacated by other girls like ourselves, we could see whoever was coming into the hall.

A group of young men wandered in and looked around. They must have decided to stay, for they were still there fifteen minutes later. All of a sudden, Betty pulled at my arm and said, "You see that tall boy over there?"

I looked and, for the first time in my life, saw Perry Saunders. Of course, he was nothing more than one of a group then. Betty, however, saw him differently. She said, as if it was something of great importance, "He's going to ask me to dance."

"Really?" I looked again and saw that this was very likely the truth. Not long afterwards I found myself standing by myself, while Betty was whizzing around the dance floor in the arms of her future husband. Not that we knew that then, I mean about the future husband – much was to happen before that came to be. Still, it did, at the time, seem like fate.

As for the rest of that evening, I remember nothing. I don't even know whether the tall boy stayed by Betty's side, or whether he walked her home, up Arden Street, or whether we all went to the ice cream shop – a restaurant really, where they whipped up delicious ice cream sundaes – to have either ice cream or a milkshake or what. I've no recollection of Perry being with us, or of when he and Betty started going together as steadies.

After a while though, everyone could see that that's what had happened. Betty was a girl who had already formed her own rules, and she made up most of the rules that went along with their relationship. This was before the sexual freedom enjoyed now by people like Betty and myself. Most of their lovemaking took place in Perry's older brother's car, and mostly there was not much more to it than kissing, or they sat on the front steps of the house and kissed. I hadn't yet got a boyfriend, but I supposed if I had one, we'd do the same.

Relationships sometimes lasted like that for years – how I do not know. Perhaps young lovers were not always as strict as we were. As a matter of fact, Betty's mother, and mine too, had more boyfriends than we had.

Anyway, we all became accustomed to having Perry around us. What happened later was a little bit hard to understand. I never ever told anyone about it. And the not-telling somehow made me feel like a kind of grown up person.

One evening, when I had been to the 'talkies' with a boy and had said good night at our front gate, I came up the steps leading to our front door and found Perry sitting on the third-top step, looking gloomy. I stopped and sat down beside him and asked what was wrong.

I don't remember what he said, but I think I must have been sympathetic because the next thing I do remember was that Perry and I had started kissing. Kiss after kiss with no thought of what we were doing. At last, thank heavens, I came to my senses, and pulling away from the last kiss, I said, "They'll be getting suspicious." I imagined that my mother or Betty's mother, whose rooms were near the front door, would have heard us shuffling our feet as we went on with what we were doing.

You might think something like that could become a

drama, with me stealing my best girlfriend's boyfriend away, ending a friendship in a very bad way.

That did not happen. When I woke up the next day, I was surprised to find I felt nothing – no guilt, no pain, no longing for more, and absolutely no wish to confess or tell anyone. For the first time in my life of twenty-one years, I had no wish to talk about what had happened.

When Perry came as usual to see Betty, he appeared to be the same to me. We greeted each other as we usually did, and not once did we look at each other as if we had a secret together.

So, in all the time that has passed, apart from in this story, I have never mentioned what took place on the front step of that house in Arden Street, and I don't believe Perry, as one half of a married couple, ever mentioned it either.

Perhaps a little spirit had got into us that evening, had we only known it. **Ψ**

Illustration: ClassicStock/Alamy Stock Photo. Photographer H. Armstrong Roberts.

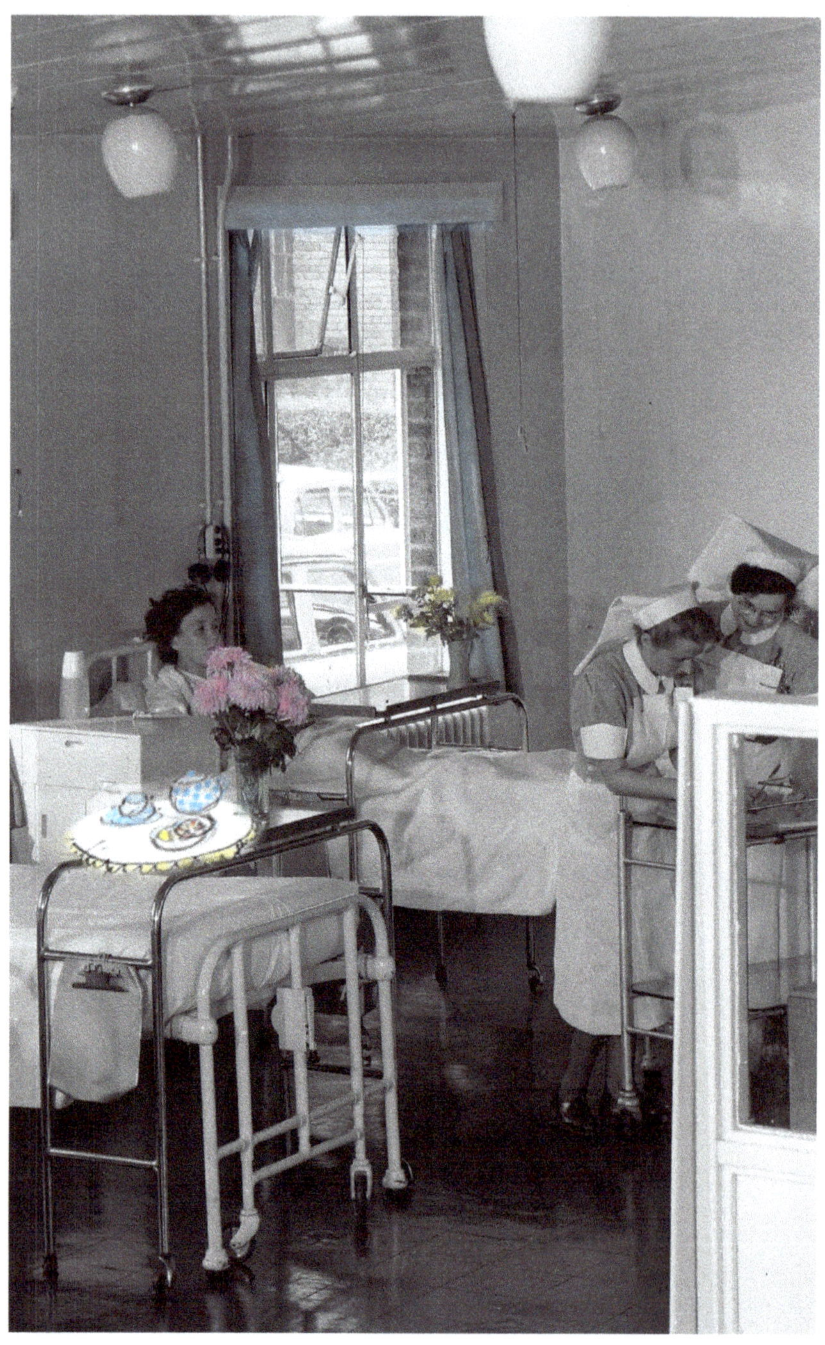

Tea on the ward

In her first year in London, Celine Preston had to go to hospital to have a little matter cleared up. She was admitted to one of the big women's hospitals somewhere near Chelsea and put to bed in what was called the Gracie Fields Ward.

Gracie Fields, a famous singer and actor, had been a patient there, and had bequeathed something delightful to all the ladies who came after her. Thanks to Gracie, a cup of tea at bedtime was a proper affair: everyone would receive her own tray, complete with teapot, cup, sugar and milk, napkin of course, and a plate with a dainty cake on it. To acknowledge Gracie's gift, the ward with its 10 beds, five on each side of the long room, was renamed in her honour.

What a lovely bequest, Celine thought, as she poured out her own cup of good strong tea. She wrote an enthusiastic letter to her mother and grandmother about it. One of her grandmother's concerns had been that Celine should be able to get a good cup of tea when she needed it.

Celine was able to enjoy this treat for three days before the orderlies came to take her to the operating room. As she lay on the stretcher being pushed along a long corridor, she found herself absorbed by an interesting pattern on the ceiling. She wondered whether it had been put there for just that reason – to distract the patients and allay any anxiety they may have had about undergoing surgery. Celine wasn't anxious though. She didn't have cancer or anything awful, just a lump that had been getting larger on the outer wall of her bladder.

Back on the ward after the surgery, Celine felt so well and strong that she was able to attend to some of the ladies wanting their hair done. The story had got around that she could, with the aid of bobby pins and a comb, set your hair before you went to sleep so you had a nice head of curly hair when you woke up the next morning. Now, despite having to stay in bed, she found she could lean over a little to one side and oblige three of them, who walked away with satisfied expressions on their faces. Regretfully she had to cancel the others in the growing queue beside her bed.

She went to sleep then, but when she woke up she discovered a worrying thing: she was unable to make her pee. After a while she became really alarmed. She complained to a nurse but nothing was done. Time was passing and she feared her bladder was going to burst!

At last the doctor on the ward must have given the order to relieve her. A nurse came with her instruments and a long white tube and proceeded to insert something into her poor suffering bladder to drain the fluid away. Not fast enough, as far as Celine was concerned – there was so much water inside, all pushing and trying at once to get into that tube and bring relief.

Thankfully nothing awful happened, and as soon as

this procedure was over Celine fell asleep again. When she woke up, the queue of straight-haired ladies had formed again, so she went on with her hair-curling favours. The work didn't seem unreasonable to Celine: she had done the same at home with her own mother.

The only person who didn't want to have her hair done was the young French woman in the next bed. She had come from Paris to take advantage of the free medical treatment for foreigners and was far too glad of that to ask for any other favours. Her condition was a mystery to the other ladies. It was something to do with her pee-pee or, worse still, her vagina, but she resented the implication that it was a sexual problem.

The elderly lady in the bed on the other side of the room had a different kind of problem. When the ambulance men had come to her home to take her away, she had not had time to arrange for the care of her cat. She sounded so sweetly fuddled when she tried to talk about it that Celine, who loved cats, was afraid the poor animal would be left to starve to death. Surely someone from the council would do something about it. She never found out whether they did or not, but she hoped so.

Eventually, the time came for Celine to have her stitches removed. This procedure had to be carefully supervised, and nearly ended in disaster for Celine. One of the nurses, who was watching closely, thought she saw one of the threads slip back into Celine's flesh. She couldn't be sure so she didn't say anything at first, but after a while her conscience pricked her and she told the matron about her concern.

That meant Celine's case had to be reassessed and another operation scheduled – with just one doctor this time – to search for a missing stitch. Sure enough, the stitch was found and extracted, causing Celine a certain amount of pain. The nurse told her later, "If I hadn't told him, it would have stayed there and given you a bad case of stitch ulcer."

By now it was nearly Christmas, and Celine found herself with a special task. She was to make a large picture of the nativity scene that was to be hung as a decoration outside in the corridor the week before Christmas.

Celine sometimes said she was born with a pair of scissors in her right hand. As a child of six or seven she had set a pattern for her life to come by inventing her own method of using those scissors. From scraps of cloth she had cut out her first doll's dress and sewn the two seams together to dress the unfortunate ragdoll in what could be called a 'shift'. Later she used her scissors in many other ways.

Although the Gracie Fields Ward was wide and long, the room next to it was quite small, with only one bed. Celine was allowed to use this room to make her nativity picture.

She spread out a large sheet of paper on the floor and set about combining her painting skills with her cutting skills. First she painted the scene of the manger on the paper; then she cut out figures of for the Madonna and child and the three kings and pasted them onto the paper. The figures cut

144

from coloured paper stood out clearly and sharply in a way that pleased the eye.

The one bed in the room was occupied by a beautiful young woman, only 25 or so years of age, who had cancer. She was already dying, although this had not yet been confirmed, and she spent parts of the precious days left to her leaning a little bit sideways to watch what Celine was doing. The other precious hours were spent sleeping or waiting for her equally beautiful husband. He came at the same time each day with their little girl, who would be six on the day before Christmas.

Celine's cut-out technique was, of course, not entirely original but as she said, no two cooks' rice puddings ever came out the same way. And the picture of the nativity pleased the child enormously. There was something of a sad fairy tale about the young husband, the beautiful wife and the innocent child. This made the cruel fate that would bring the story to an end even more poignant. Celine wondered whether the child would grow up with memories of her mother.

In any event, the nativity picture was a success. Attached to a rod, it was hung above the corridor from strings attached to the walls at either end, and seemed to wave about a little and fan people as they passed under it going about their business.

After Christmas, Celine and three other patients were dressed warmly and taken to the train station, where they were installed in a private carriage and sent on their way to the hospital's convalescent home by the sea in Hastings. There they slept soundly in their beds for by night, and spent their days going for walks, looking at stone ruins and finding out about what had happened in Hastings on that day in 1066.

On New Year's Eve, Celine was given the job of painting funny faces on balloons for some ye olde English merrie-making. Matron was pleased: it wasn't often she had a real live artist in her power. They stayed for two weeks, until officially convalesced.

Back in London, although discharged and quite cured, Celine was regularly invited to the Gracie Fields Ward for visits. When Matron walked into the ward one day and saw her eating dinner on the edge of the French girl's bed, her expression said, "Oh and what's going on here?"

But she knew perfectly well what was going on. There was no need for anyone to hide Celine under the bedclothes: she was a welcome visitor. She would even set a few pincurls while she was there, in return for a slice of cake from a Gracie Fields' tea tray. Ψ

Illustration: Not actually the Chelsea Women's Hospital, but the Montague Hospital in Mexborough, South Yorkshire, 1959. Photo by Michael Walters. Heritage Image Partnership Ltd/Alamy. Tea set drawing by Eileen Kramer.

The glove counter

It was not so long ago that ladies wore gloves, and in New York you were likely to have had the pleasure of buying these at glove counters such as the one at Tiffany's, on the corner of 5th Avenue and 57th Street. Glove counters made the business of replacing your old crumpled-looking gloves very pleasant.

First of all you were given a stool to sit on. Then you leaned lightly against the glass display case. The next move was to place your elbow on the counter – sometimes you got a little cushion to rest on – with your arm in a straight vertical line and your hand waiting gently, hopefully, pointing skyward, tensed in readiness for the first onslaught of the black leather finger to come. With a firm pulling motion, the shop assistant coaxed the fine leather – from which poor animal you didn't know – down towards the hand itself, stretching and smoothing until there it was: a lovely elegant leather-clad finger. The remaining fingers soon followed until the whole hand was enclosed by the glove, with a small hole as part of its design revealing a little of the back of the hand, just before the fingers began, to be felt rather than seen. So elegant.

Eileen always bought her gloves at Tiffany's. On one particular occasion, she struck up a conversation with another lady receiving the same attention. This lady was not very tall: it wasn't as easy for her to get her elbow into position as it had been for Eileen. The lady didn't mind though. She smiled a lot with her exotic sort of mouth and her white teeth. She looked glamorous in a conservative kind of way. She seemed pleased too, with something about her own being.

She told Eileen who she was, but not for everyone else to hear − she was just a simple person after all. But still, she was Gloria Swanson, the silent movie actress, and star of *Sunset Boulevard*. As they started to talk, you'd never have known that she was one of the most famous actors in the movie world. She was so friendly and nice to talk to.

Eileen said she was tired of her baggy old gloves. Gloria said she was too.

Just then a man came along, well dressed and good-looking, about 50, Eileen supposed. The sales girl who was looking after Eileen whispered that he was one of the directors of Tiffany's. "He comes here for breakfast," she whispered.

Another sales girl had brought gloves for Gloria to try. They sat there, elbows on the little velvet cushions and fingers pointing skywards, and the fitting began.

The man stayed to watch for a while. He said, "Miss Katie is the best fitter." Miss Katie, Eileen's sales girl, looked pleased.

Gloria Swanson said, "My mother has always made my clothes."

"Very nice too, I'm sure," said the man.

"I've always made my own," Eileen said.

"You'd be a clever lady," he said. "I can't make my own

shirts. I be no good at all."

"What are you good at?" Eileen asked. "You must be good at something."

"I be good at playing golf. I also read books."

"Oh, have you ever heard of a writer named H Rider Haggard?" Gloria said. "He's very good. He wrote a book called *She*."

"I know that one," Eileen said. "Someone also made a movie of it. A group of people went in search of the woman they called 'She'."

"You be a movie star," the director of Tiffany's said, turning to Gloria. "Were you in that movie? I remember it well. They all had to fight their way through the jungle to get to her palace – I mean the 'She' woman."

"No, I was not," said Gloria. "But you might have seen me in *Sunset Boulevard*."

"Oh, yes!" said the director of Tiffany's. "Can you say, 'I'm ready for my close-up, Mr De Mille'?"

"Ah, that line – after I'd walked down the stairs at the end. Everyone gets it wrong." And Gloria dipped her chin gracefully, turned her head to show the director her profile and said softly, "Alright Mr De Mille, I'm ready for my close-up."

The director of Tiffany's clapped his hands and said to Eileen, "She would have been good as the 'She' lady wouldn't she."

Eileen tried to imagine Gloria in the mysterious abode of H Rider Haggard's *She*, but no: Gloria was too modern – not 'contemporary' but of that era when Modern Dance began in the romantic city of Viennese waltzes.

"I don't think Miss Swanson would be right for 'She'," Eileen replied. "She was supposed to be 2000 years old."

"And would you be an actor too?" he said. "You don't be Greta Garbo!"

"I'd like to be, but I'm not. Thank you for asking," said Eileen.

"Look after these two ladies," the director of Tiffany's said to Katie and continued on his way to breakfast.

Katie went on smoothing the glove over Eileen's first finger and the other assistant did the same to Gloria's finger.

"Did your mother make the clothes for your first film test?" Eileen asked.

"Yes," said Gloria, and went off into a dream remembering what it was like. "It was blue. I told my mother not to put buttons on it. Anyway, it worked didn't it?" She looked wistful as the assistant massaged the finger of the glove all the way down her flesh-and-blood finger.

"Where do you think that man came from?" Eileen said. "There were lots of 'be' this and 'be' that."

"We think he's from Yorkshire in England," the glove assistant said.

"He made me go all York-ish myself," Eileen said. "The *New* York sort. I be from West 57th Street."

Gloria laughed. And they both went back to concentrating on their glove fitting.

After a while they decided on their purchases and found themselves together outside Tiffany's, with their new gloves wrapped in tissue in neat little packages. As they waited to cross Fifth Avenue, Gloria seemed loathe to leave her new acquaintance so they began to walk down West 57th Street, Eileen providing a running commentary on the locale, which was unfamiliar to Gloria.

First they went past the fabric store – the best in Manhattan, said Eileen, which interested Gloria greatly – then they passed the Italian restaurant where they made their own spaghetti sauce. Pausing outside Carnegie Hall, on the corner of 7th Avenue, Eileen explained that her apartment was a bit further down, in a building where Frank Sinatra had once hosted parties in the roof garden restaurant. Beyond that was the Art Students League, where Eileen was said to be one of the best models. And if they kept going down all the way to the end of the street, they would come to the Hudson River waterfront, where great sea-going vessels docked.

They had turned back by now and soon came to the Russian Tea Room. "How enchanting!" cried Gloria. "You must let me take you to lunch!" Eileen hesitated at first, although she was by now quite hungry, but Gloria insisted, so they went in, had good bowls of borscht, and Russian dumplings and caviar and talked about many things.

All in all, Eileen considered the day had been most successful, thanks to the Tiffany's glove counter. Ψ

Illustration: Gloria Swanson (detail from photo of Gloria Swanson with Barbara Stanwyk). Background drawing by Eileen Kramer.

Actors

When I was very young and had no sense, I believed in the myth of the talent spotter: that you might be sitting in a café, spending your last cents on a coffee, thinking you might have to go back home to some place like Ohio – because this would be in America – and eat humble pie and admit you'd been wrong and not cut out to be an actor, when suddenly – bang, crash, wallop – a talent scout sidles up and asks you to take a screen test for some wonderful film like *Gone with the Wind*.

The truth is, this happened to me right here in Sydney. The scout was a woman, and she liked my hat, which she said made me look like a Shakespearean character out of *Much Ado about Nothing*. Wide-eyed and utterly ignorant, I agreed to go to the 'studio' – actually a room in the Coogee Bay Hotel – and read for the director of a new film. I didn't quite believe it would lead to anything and I was right, for I must have been so terrible, despite the feather in my hat, that the casting agent was sure to have lost her job for wasting the director's time. He dismissed me with an irritated grunt, but I didn't mind very much. I suppose it was a lesson not to wear that hat again.

Anyway, that was a long time ago, before I became a dancer and started to understand such things a little better.

More recently, when a casting director approached me about being in a television series, I still had some misgivings. I was a little suspicious about his motives and didn't want to be in movies by then anyway. But my adviser, Tracey Spring, a filmmaker herself, said, "Why not?" and somehow I found myself sitting in my friend Sue Healey's kitchen, one of those fateful rooms where great things are planned, letting this man, this casting director, take shots of me saying what I considered to be uninteresting things like, "Maybe I should get some birds." What? Why birds? Both Tracey and Sue just laughed and offered the man some coffee.

But I must have done something right, because several weeks later, Tracey and I found ourselves sitting on a plane bound for Queensland. Not quite as glamorous as Hollywood – but it was nice to know we'd be seeing the Gold Coast.

When we arrived, a nice young woman was waiting for us. She said she and her car were to be at our disposal while we were there. Her name was Louise. She told us she lived on the Gold Coast with her partner and loved it.

Louise took us to an apartment, which she said would be our home for the next five days. It was surprisingly large, with two bedrooms, each with its own little bathroom, a TV room, and a large living room with a kitchen bar where we could have breakfasts and cook anything we liked.

It was too late to go to the studio to work so Louise took Tracey to the market where she did some food shopping. We were able to make dinner, and we ate it sitting on one

of our two balconies – the one from my bedroom, overlooking the bay. Tracey's overlooked the ocean.

Our building was one of many on this part of the Gold
Coast. "It's just like a forest," I had remarked to Tracey
when we arrived. "A forest of concrete and steel." It was,
however, very pleasant to sit so high up, looking at the vast-
ness of the sea.

The next morning, Louise came again to pick us up. We
first went to another apartment, more like a small house
with a front garden, as it was on the ground floor – apparently just one of a row of such buildings the film company
had rented. This was not the set where we were to work
that day. It was just somewhere for me to rest while not
actually shooting.

A woman came to make me up for the scene to be shot
that morning, and I was taken to the set by a young man
named Jimmy, who seemed to pop up from nowhere. To
get there, I had to walk with him along a very rough path.
They had given me a walker because the way was so un-
even, but I hid it behind a bush and said to Jimmy, "Now
we can walk."

Jimmy smiled and at that moment something, somehow,
snapped. From then on, it was as if Jimmy and I were together, set apart from the other members of the film company. It was quite unspoken, simply a feeling. Jimmy may
have been new there. I really didn't have to think about it.

Anyway, he escorted me to a place that looked like the
long veranda of a hotel. There were rows of chairs, so I

assumed I would be required to sit in one of them. While I stood thinking about this, other people began to arrive, and as they sat in the chairs, I did the same. We actors were all in this together. Another actor stood facing us, while the director, who also seemed to pop up out of nowhere, got ready to give him his direction. Someone else gave him his lines.

That turned out to be only a rehearsal, and we had to wait for someone else to pop up. This turned out to be an attractive woman, a well-known actress, or so the man in the next chair told me.

My job was to notice this woman as she took her seat in the row in front of me. This was my great moment. I did it with great feeling − almost too great, I should say now, thinking back on it − as if a visitor from Jupiter or Mars had come to be among us. The director didn't object so I held onto that feeling while the next thing happened, which was some lines said by the actor standing before us. He was asked to do it a number of times but didn't seem to satisfy the director, and I couldn't help wondering whether his feelings were hurt.

At this point the director was called away. We were all left in mid air so to speak and everyone became a bit silly. Apparently the man had been required to say forcefully, "Who do you think you are?" So everyone began asking each other the same question with different emphases: "And *who* do you think you *are*?" "And who *do* you think you are?" "And who do *you* think you are?" My neighbour

– the one who'd been telling me what to do – looked at me and said, "Who do you think *you* are?" To which I replied just as foolishly, "I don't know. Who do *you* think I am?"

Far back, beyond range of the camera, I could see someone asking Jimmy who he thought he was, and, if I could trust my lip reading skills, I thought I saw him say, "I'm Jimmy; who are you?"

When the director came back everyone became sensible again, and the actor discovered he should have said, not "*Who* are you?" but "*What* are you that you could allow such a thing to happen?"

We did some more takes and I gave the famous actress my Jupiter or Mars incredulous look and hoped they got the shot. Then it was over and we all went to a nice buffet lunch.

Tracey meanwhile had had time to attend to all her emails.

The next scene was later that day. Jimmy escorted me to another apartment with a garden that was supposed to be my own home. People were coming for afternoon tea. The table was already set. They were to be seen walking up the path toward my front door. Demonstrating once again what an amazing actor I was, I went to the window, lifted the curtain a little, and looked out to watch for them. What I (but not the camera) actually saw out the window was a back yard with a garbage can, two dead potted plants and a shed. But I must have been convincing enough.

Tracey and I had a great vegetable casserole, looked at

the ocean and went to our own beds.

On the last day, Jimmy escorted me to the car park and as I was about to leave him, I said impulsively, "I'll never forget you, Jimmy."

He replied, "And I'll never forget you."

I hope, if he ever reads this, he'll know it's true: I've never forgotten him. Ψ

Illustration: Photograph of Eileen courtesy of Anca Frankenhaeuser; and setup for (unrelated) film shoot, Gold Coast Studio.

The resident

Ellie Longfield, resident of the Good Life aged care home in a seaside suburb in Queensland, had been given a new mattress because the old one had lost its straight and narrow shape. The handyman who had brought it to her room had draped it over the back of Ellie's chair while he removed the old mattress. Looking at it hanging there limply made Ellie think of Salvador Dali's dripping clock, which hung floor-ward in the same heavy sensuous way.

This observation was all very interesting, but Ellie had something else on her mind, namely the affair of the new resident.

The nurse had brought him into the sitting room that morning, pushing the huge padded chair in which he sat, slightly hunched. He was a large, broad-shouldered man, broad all over it seemed, as he not only filled the chair but overflowed it as well. Ellie really only saw him from the back and a little to the side, but she noticed that he had a side parting in his rich-looking white hair and that it had been swept or combed from the parting over to the left side of his forehead. It looked, she said to herself, attractive. That was all. She hadn't seen any more of his head or his face.

The nurse must have told him she would be happy to take him further into the room, but he indicated with a shrug that he was content to stay at this end, near the cups and saucers, and tea and coffee machines.

Ellie thought to herself that he must be a new resident, perhaps a bit glum about having to face the fact that he could no longer care for himself. There was no one with him but the nurse, so maybe he didn't have a wife, or children. He looked like a solo kind of man.

Only mildly interested, she didn't think or imagine anything else, although when the nurse left, Ellie didn't recall her saying, as nurses usually did, "I'll be back."

So there was this large broad-shouldered mass of humanity left in the famous residents' sitting room, all alone, and not even a cup of coffee on the table in front of him.

Ellie had finished her own cup and was not interested in staying any longer. She had lots of things to plan. Her work, which she was able to go ahead with even though she lived in the Good Life residence, depended almost entirely on her imagination. And at this time, her mind was full of it. She didn't tend to get involved with the affairs of other residents. If they found her stand-offish, she didn't care: when they saw the results of her isolated way of living among them, they might understand.

She gathered her belongings together and would have been off, away to her room, had something not stopped her. It was the big man in the stuffed chair. He was coughing and stopping and coughing again and again.

Ellie stood still, sympathetic. She too sometimes had to cough, and she knew what it was like if you needed a tissue but couldn't find the box. She looked around, and

164

seeing no tissues on the coffee table, she put down her stuff and went to the shelves. Still not seeing any tissues, she whipped several sheets of paper towel out of the dispenser near the sink, took them to the table and put them down for the new resident.

She heard him say "thank you" in quite a pleasing voice, and his hand came forward to take them. But he couldn't quite reach, so, with a gesture even she herself felt was solicitous, she moved the papers a little closer. Thus, for one brief moment, he and she were united in that simple objective. She didn't even think of looking up at his face.

Having done what she could to relieve him should he need to cough again, she picked up her belongings and left by the doorway at the end of the kitchen counter. That was all there was to it.

The next afternoon, however, she realised, with a sense of 'Why didn't I …?' that she had no idea what sort of face he had. Her imagination went to work, creating all sorts of images: kindly eyes, firm but sensual mouths, strong chins and whole faces like Gregory Peck or other such examples of strong and tenderly humorous manhood.

It was tantalising. Why she hadn't looked up when she had made that small human gesture? She began to invent charming or tender glances or even little incidents that would happen between them – some richness of emotion or connection of spirit. A physical relationship was not at all likely. Ellie had to consider all the other ways of together-ness that might happen, once she had seen his face.

This was her one regret: she had not looked up at his face. She couldn't spend all her time by the tea and coffee machine in case he should ever be brought there again. She couldn't go up to each floor hoping to find him in one of the rooms, and she couldn't even ask at the reception desk for him. It was a large establishment and she may never even see him in the distance, passing away into an elevator. In the end, she told herself not to be silly: it was good to do a tiny kind deed without looking to see what effect you were having on the other person.

It was then that Janet, one of the nursing assistants, came in with the handyman and the new mattress. Ellie was pleased about that, despite being distracted by the way it flowed over the back of the chair, but she couldn't help telling Janet all about the mysterious resident. "I think it would make a good story," she added.

Janet agreed. Then to Ellie's surprise, Janet said, "You mentioned a broad-shouldered sort of person?"

"Yes!" Ellie exclaimed, with fresh hope surging through her bosom. "With white hair swept to one side."

"Yes," Janet replied, "And would it have been last Friday?"

"Yes, it would – last Friday!" She wasn't actually sure but she wanted it to be, and was amazed when Janet responded with: "A new resident answering that description did indeed arrive last Friday."

Ellie felt excited and glad, but also a sort of let down: the mystery might be gone. Of course, she had to know.

"What was he like?" she asked.

Janet's reply made things worse in a way. She said, as though it was the only thing about him that mattered, "He had a big bushy moustache right across his lip."

Ellie could never ever imagine kissing a man with a bushy moustache. She visualised it, all the way across his mouth. How could you even find the mouth, she felt, in order to kiss him? Disappointed yet ever hopeful, Ellie's imagination searched for the kind of relationship you could have with such a man as that.

A few days later, Ellie saw Janet and asked her how the gentleman with the bushy moustache was liking it at the Good Life residence.

"I didn't say bushy," she replied. "I said it went straight across his lip."

"Oh," said Ellie, "So, you could see where his lips were." She thought of the great Ronald Coleman, an actor everyone loved, who had a charming moustache and a wonderful smile. Ronald Coleman was in a film called *Lost Horizon,* in which people lived fabulous lives and never grew old. Ellie wondered whether the new resident looked anything like that. She wasn't hoping for a romance, but merely wanted to know what kind of man he was.

As she and Janet were standing there in the upstairs corridor, they had to move aside to allow two nurses to pass, pushing a strange-looking apparatus towards the bathroom. It was a tall thing, with a small platform for standing on, and two handlebars to support a person in a standing position while they were taken to the shower room. The person would therefore be obliged to take a heroic forward-looking kind of stance, and hang on for his own safety.

As it passed, Ellie recognised the figure, now very sparsely clad, as the man whose face she had not seen. Standing up like that, holding onto the handlebars, looking noble and so on, he gave the impression of being a Roman charioteer, not someone being taken to the shower.

This only deepened her resolve to get a good look at his face one day, and find out whether there was any hope of establishing a connection – not sexually of course; hopefully just an interesting relationship with someone who looked like Ronald Coleman or at least Gregory Peck.

A few days later, she was making herself a coffee in the sitting room, when a woman came up beside her. The woman was coughing quite a lot, and as she took a plate from the stack beside the coffee machine, she apologised to Ellie, adding, "It's not a virus cough, you know."

"Even so," replied Ellie, "it must be very uncomfortable for you."

She watched the woman pick out two cakes, and make her way back to a table near the door to the veranda, where a figure in a big padded chair was sitting. All she could see of the figure was the back of his head, with white hair, parted neatly on the side.

"It's him," she thought. "And that must be his wife."

She considered going over to introduce herself, but then

she stopped herself. Maybe not. She realised she didn't actually want to see his face at all.

Much better to hold onto the mystery. That way, he could be Ronald Coleman forever. And a Roman charioteer as well. Ψ

Illustration: Ronald Coleman in Under Two Flags, *with Claudette Colbert. Twentieth Century Fox, 1936. Pictorial Press Ltd/Alamy Stock Photo.*

Room 8

Room 8 is off a long corridor with ten bedrooms on either side. Halfway down is the nurses' station, where the nurses and nurses aides gather. The cleaners also sometimes linger there but not for long – there is no idling the time away. With mops, dusters and wet rags – well, not rags it must be said, but neat little cleaning clothes – they pass through like a small hurricane, making everything absolutely spotless.

Anyway, apart from those people, nurses and all, you hardly ever see anyone in the corridor, not even visitors. If visitors come they need to have their temperature taken and provide proof of flu vaccination, which is a very good thing, considering the coronavirus and the lockdown restrictions. For once, it seems everyone understands that we are all in this thing together.

Mostly the doors of the rooms along the corridor are left open, although you don't turn your head as you walk past, not wanting to seem curious. Most occupants are awakened early, showered and given breakfast, which is usually very good, and after that would go somewhere, either in a bus with others to see the sights of Sydney, or to exercise class or down to the garden room where they can, if they wish, make their own coffee or tea.

While they are away, you can look right into their rooms as far as the wide window to the outside. You can see the treetops almost touching the glass.

Seeing the shiny floor of one of those rooms one day, and the tree tops waving about in the breeze, you wish you could use it for a dance film you are thinking about: floor work, with two dancers curled up with foreheads touching the floor, opening up like flowers in bloom. You ask Maria who is in charge of all new admissions and she says yes, if the room is not occupied, that's fine. And you forget for a moment about Room 8.

Room 8 is a mystery. If you do happen to catch a tiny detail, it is of the bed, with its long slim legs reflected in the lovely clear shiny floor, and the suggestion of a human form under the covers. You don't know whose form it is – man or woman – or what is wrong with the person lying so quietly there. All you have had is a quick glimpse.

And then it comes to pass that the nurse says to you one evening, "May I ask you something?" She speaks softly as though it is something secretive she has to say. "I wonder whether you would be kind enough to have dinner this evening with Susan in Room 8."

You are surprised. Why? She doesn't explain, but you get the idea. Susan is the person in bed in Room 8. Obviously, she can't leave her bed and the nurse is being kind, in fact quite tender in the way she speaks. Of course, you say you'd love to. The idea appeals to you. And some of the mystery of Room 8 is explained.

The nurse says she will come and get you when the time comes. You feel pleased and do your hair nicely in honour of the occasion. You walk into the room and she is lying propped up with a pillow. She looks cool and calm and very pretty. The nurse has already told you that Susan had once been a fashion model. Having known a few fashion models – 'girls' as they were called in Paris, where your friend Percival worked in the world of high fashion – you can imagine it's true of this woman, who looks quite young; you feel you've known her before. You say, "Oh, here is the model girl!"

"That was a long time ago," she replies, smiling as she speaks. Something about her cool calm manner tells you that she no longer frets over the past.

While we wait for dinner to be brought in you look at two paintings on the wall. You feel sure they are in some way connected with her modelling days. One is of a fashionable woman wearing a red gown and a large hat tilted so high on one side that you know at once which period it comes from: those days of the great French designers – creators of style and ways of life that affected many people you knew, before World War II changed so many things. A world of the past.

You wonder whether the painting of the sophisticated model is of Susan herself. She doesn't say so, just quietly smiles, moving only her head, for Susan cannot move any part of her body except her head. Thank goodness she can eat.

You sit with her and eat your dinner, and as you eat you tell her the story of the sad monkey, which has already been told within these pages. You tell her about Percival, who came as she did from Queensland and became such a success in the world of high fashion in Paris, meeting all the great designers and indeed many other famous people. You think Susan may have known him.

You ask if you might take a photo on your phone to give to your editor, who's helping with the book of stories you've been writing. You think the painting of the model in the red gown and the fantastically tilted hat could be turned into an illustration for your sad monkey story.

This is the way things happen: you create something but it is never quite the way you want it to be; then without even trying, along comes something that looks so very right!

As you are about to ask Susan's permission to use the painting, the nurse enters the room and whispers to you that you must not stay any longer, because the doctor is coming to perform a "little operation" on Susan.

Disappointed, you leave Room 8, but you feel hopeful: surely Susan will say yes. She has been in that room or others like it for a very long time. Ψ

Illustration: A room not dissimilar to Room 8. Photograph Catherine Gray..

The garden party

The house was called 'Greenfield'. It had been built before the war between the North and the South, by a Colonel in the confederate army, Colonel Greenfield, and furnished slowly, by people who knew a lot about early American furniture and precious carpets and curtains. The people who lived there were proud of it. The rooms were never untidy and hardly anything took place that was not in keeping with the genre, style and air of the interiors. Even when the members of the family died, and the house eventually became the home of another family with a different name, the style never changed.

No changes were ever made until one day the lady of the house, who was very conservative and had carefully kept everything the same, died. Her husband, whose name was James, was left alone in the house.

James didn't mind being alone very much. He went out every day to sit in the barbershop and chat with other men in similar situations. He prepared his own dinner of a good steak, but no vegetables unfortunately, and then looked at the tele. If he was lonely, he didn't notice it. He had a man named Henry who looked after his clothes and things.

After some time had passed, he met a young woman named Eva from the city and they fell in love.

Once a week James and Eva and a lady called Mary Lou, who owned the local historical society, went on discovery car drives through the valleys and mountains of West Virginia. On these trips they saw much of interest that was happening on the land, such as people building their own houses or digging with huge earthmoving machines. Once they saw a man using one of these machines to move a hill from one side of a long country road to the other. They watched until this had been accomplished and then the three of them applauded him for his masterly handling of the great machine. There were many such things that made their drives so interesting.

Sometimes, when Mary Lou couldn't come, James and Eva went alone, and these trips were of a more romantic nature.

On one such occasion James and Eva spent quite a long time parked on the side of a forest of purple azalea trees, getting to know more about each other – this being before she went to live with him. Beyond the trees was a delightful stream, its water sparkling in the sunlight.

When they returned to the town and turned from the main road into the side street where he lived, they saw things going on that alarmed them. A large furniture van, an ambulance and a fire engine, were parked with their drivers and other people making a mess on the beautiful orderly front lawn of the house. Two firemen rose up through a hole in the roof while other firemen were coming and going through the front doorway. All the signs of a fire were there, except that they saw no flames.

James stopped the car and said, "My house is on fire!"

Then he seemed to go into shock.

Eva replied, "No, it can't be yours; it's always some other house down the street."

But it was indeed his house, so James recovered enough to get out and go to speak to the fireman.

Eva stayed watching in the car, until after a while somebody came to say that James had asked him to drive her home. This surprised her because he wasn't usually so thoughtful. However, she went back to her apartment, not far away at all, and spent the rest of the evening wondering what was taking place.

The fire had not engulfed the whole house, but had made a hole in the kitchen ceiling so that some of the furniture in the room above fell through. The rest of the house, with its early American treasures and its priceless carpets, was stained by smoke. It was uninhabitable, so James had to go and live for a while in apartment on the main road – not in a tall apartment building but in the back part of someone else's house.

About six weeks later James was able to return to his own freshly painted and restored house, but the emotional shock had affected him and not long after that he asked Eva to come and live with him.

His daughter said confidentially to her, "If you want to marry dad, you'll have to ask him; he never does anything unless he is asked."

"Then he will do it," she added.

But Eva made no move on that and it was not until a

few weeks later, when James had an attack of something, that she eventually went to live with him.

They were happy together. She understood everything about the house and was careful not to disturb the even tenor of his ways, except that she included vegetables in his evening meal and sometimes made blueberry pie, which he liked very much.

One day, however, a friend of Eva's named Jeanie came to stay for a week. She was a well-known artist and, wishing to give James and Eva a little present, she painted a portrait of Eva and gave it to them when she was leaving. It was a good professional work of art, not an amateur piece, so Eva felt it should be framed properly and hung on a wall. James had no problem with that, except he didn't want it on one of *their* walls because it was not an early American portrait. Eva could see he had a painful decision to make, for he didn't want to offend her by hiding the picture away in the back of a closet. Eva decided she was tired of being treated as a non-person and said as much to James. In the end he got Henry to have it framed and hung in the small breakfast room where he would see it only if he looked sideways.

By this time the back garden with its fish pond and other features was restored and the lawn looked fresh and lovely. Eva said to James, "I think we should have a garden party," and he agreed.

Eva had become friendly with the members of the local Trillium Performing Arts Collective, so she asked several of the dancers to help stage a ballet in the garden. James agreed to this too, and within a few weeks she had choreographed a dance performance about people dancing at a garden party – a play within a play as it were. But she had a problem: she didn't have enough dancers to play the party guests. So what had she to do? She had to make some: was she not a hands-on choreographer?

She used some strong muslin for the figures: cutting, sewing and stuffing them; sewing eyes and lips, arms and legs, heads, and feet in little pointed white satin shoes. The ladies wore long empire style gowns and large hats. The man – only one, sad to say – was well dressed too, in a tweed hat and stiff white collar. He was clearly able to sit beside his wife in her elegant costume, while their two daughters, Betty Lou and Mary Ellen, stood beside them. Not a crowd, but enough to represent a garden party, and as one of the dancers said, "Less is more."

The party was a success and James's cousin, who had been invited, said it was a pity the whole town couldn't have come. Some were said to be jealous because they had not been asked.

That was all very fine, but Eva now had a problem. She could see that it pained James to have these four 1905 people sitting for the rest of their lives, and his life too, in the priceless Early American parlour. Their kind, from 1905, was not his kind.

Eventually, their friend Mary Lou from the historical society, solved that problem. She found a home for them in the early American show-parlour of the historical society and they spent their days there representing the Queen of Bulgaria or some other European country and her family, who had once embarked on a royal tour of the United States.

This relieved James, and he spent the rest of his life with Eva, enjoying that lovely Early American Scarlett O'Hara kind of house. Ψ

Illustration: The lifesize figures created by Eileen to fill out the numbers at Bill's garden party, Lewisburg, West Virginia. The photo shows them in their final roles as visiting royalty in the 'show parlour' of the local historical society.

Sex & grammar

In a park near a house with a shed, a man was standing on a box handing out tickets to homeless people who needed space for various reasons. The main reason, it seemed, was to have sex. That's what they said: 'have sex'. The man looked at them scornfully.

"Youse can't have no sex, here or anywhere," he said gruffly to the first young couple in the queue. "No one can have sex here, nor anywhere, so forget about it, youse two."

"Why can't we? We're as good as anyone else."

"You may be good but that's not the point. I'm telling youse, you just can't *have* sex here, nor anywhere else. So don't ask unless you ask properly."

"I think you're awful. Why can't we? I'm gonna call the police. It's permitted now, you should know that." That was the young man talking. The girl then piped up and cried, "Yes, I wanna know why. Eric tell him: I wanna know why we can't have sex."

"If you don't know I ain't gonna tell you," the man said. Then he looked alarmed and shouted out because they'd moved away and he could see where they were headed: the grass.

"Hey, not on our lovely grass, you can't! Get back here and wait your turn."

They had only been pretending and came back. "Yeah,

well, people will get impatient with you, Mr You-up-there-on-that-box, Mr Thank-you-thank-you-I'm-so-wonderful-just-because-I-have-all-that-space-to-give-out!'".

A middle-aged couple nearby looked haughty. Real high and mighty they were. Even so, they too wanted space for sex.

"My good man, why can't we all behave like civilised people? All we want is a little time, and space too, I don't mind saying. Now be a good fellow, and stop fooling around."

He took his lady friend's hand and kissed it.

"Here, none of that. Wait till I give you leave to make love to this lady."

"I don't want leave. I want to have sex," said the lady, prim and proper.

"You see, you're all the same. You say you want to *have* sex and I say you can't."

A lot of people wanting sex began to get angry.

"You silly old toad, what do you know about sex? I'll bet you couldn't do it if you tried," cried one belligerent-looking woman.

"Yeah, I bet you couldn't either," yelled her partner, a sexy-looking gigolo.

"You're right; I couldn't because no one can. It can't be *done*," replied the man with a look that suggested he had superior knowledge of what could be done and what couldn't. "Anyway, I understand you can't wait. But you have to. Those people got here first."

186

He handed two tickets to the first young couple, and pointed to the ramshackle wooden shed down the end of the garden where all this was taking place.

"There you are. Now once you get inside, I know what you want to do…"

"So do we! Come on, let's go!" cried the young man.

"I know what you want and I'm only too happy to give you two tickets, but I tell you, you can't have sex. It's not possible, not unless you learn the right way to ask. But anyway, leave the place as you found it. It's neat and tidy except for a few crusts on the floor from yesterday. They'll get eaten by the rats but not while you're in there, so don't worry. Off you go and don't let don't be too long. Others are waiting."

He sat back on his box looking relieved, while the couple took the two tickets and made straight for the wooden shed. They opened the door and went in. The waiting couples fidgeted and whispered to each other.

At this point another man entered. His name was Reggie. He was the owner of the house and the wooden shed.

"Give it a break, Ron," he said. "Why don't you tell them why they can't have sex?"

"Why should I tell them? I'm sick to death of people saying they'll *have* sex all over the country. It's a question of grammar," said Ron a little sulkily.

"Well, your own grammar is not always so good; look at yourself," said Reggie.

Ron looked down sadly. "Yes, I suppose you're right."

"Of course he's right," cried one of the group of homeless people waiting for their turn to use the wooden shed. They were all becoming troublesome.

Ron looked up again, not wanting to be put down by these sex-crazed people. They were all homeless that was their trouble. "No one wants …" he said to himself. Here Ron paused, realising he had been about to say "No one wants to have their sex out in the open in the Sydney Domain," so he reformed his sentence and found another way. "No one wants to perform the sexual act," he paused again, searching, knowing that what he had said to himself sounded unbearably pompous. So how else, with all the words in the English language, could he say it? His friend was right anyway: his own grammar was pretty awful.

The trouble was he had fallen into bad habits. He tried to blame his jobs – like the present one handing out unofficial permits for people to use his friend's wooden shed for their sex needs. Again, he pulled himself up: what had he just said – 'sex needs'? He tried another way: 'for their need to …' – what? To give way to the need to what? To submit to the demands of sexual desire? That wasn't what he wanted to say either.

The impatient couple at the head of the line of homeless people started harassing the others saying that the government ought to provide proper accommodation for them, not someone's broken-down old shed.

He had to admit the man was right. People needed some privacy. Especially for their sex needs. There it was again: their 'sex needs'! Sex wasn't a thing you *needed*. It wasn't something you *did* or *had* or *would have*. It was what you were, like a man or a woman. You were of the male sex or the female sex. You couldn't go around *having* sex.

His friend Reggie was kind and understanding enough to let these poor homeless people use his shed. Next week when the repairs to his house were done, would he let them use his house? That was the question: how far could you go with your kindness?

And so it went on all afternoon. People demanding their sex rights. sex scandals, sex in the churches, sex in the railroad department, sex in hospital wards, sex in public housing, even in big department stores, and worst of all, sex in parliament. Ron had really got something to complain about with that last one.

Eventually he found himself thinking about himself and sex. What was going on inside the wooden shed? To his own mortification he found himself thinking those words he complained of — I'd like to 'have sex'!

It was a shock and for a while he was depressed. Then gradually he started remembering things, like a girl he knew who had told him how she'd been treated. A man she had always admired had taken her out in a car, stopped it in a lonely place, and said "What you need is a good screw!"

"Men!" she had said. "That is not the way to talk about something so sacred as sex."

Another girl had told him about something that had happened to her in Pakistan — girls liked telling him such things: she had made the mistake of going for a drive with a man and he had stopped the car, also in a lonely place and said, without any reason so she thought, looking at a thick clump of bushes, "Let's go out there and get naked." Of course, she didn't!

Meanwhile, the homeless people had formed a protest march, from the front gate to the box where he was standing. "Give us our sex rights." "Better accommodation for sex."

He groaned: they still ignored the rules of grammar. But what could they have said instead?

Furthermore, he began to feel the need himself and thought about Reggie's sister, to whom he'd been paying attention recently. The need grew and grew and he took out his mobile phone and called her. After a lot of unnecessary talk, he knew he had to say it.

"Mabel," he said a bit sheepishly. "I'm thinking of you all the time. I want to see you."

"Why?" Mabel asked, knowing full well what he wanted. "Don't say you're in love with me!"

He groaned for the second time that day. "Yes Mabel. I think I am. I was about to say 'I want to screw you' but instead I want to say, 'I want you, Mabel. I want to make love to you'." There it was, out in an ordinary plainspoken old-fashioned way: "I want to make love."

Mabel made a little squeaking sound of delight. "Oh, you mean you want to have sex with me!" she said. "I'll be there in a minute."

Just then his friend Reggie came along and asked what was wrong.

"It's your sister," he moaned. "She's just like everyone else: she thinks sex is something you can *have*. I give up!" Ψ

Illustration: Montage by Catherine Gray from Allamy stock photographs.

The no-hair people

The no-hair people lived in a remote part of the country across the river and on the other side of the mountain. Hardly anyone from Bushy-Hair Town ever went to No-Hair Land. If they did, they came back with no hair and everyone shunned them.

Perce Mullens, for example, was a bit put out one day when he was stopped in the street by a man with no hair.

"Hi Perce," said the man. "How are ya?"

"I don't know you," Perce replied. "You look like one of them no-hair people to me."

"You do know me, Perce," replied the man. "I'm Ed Pringle."

"Don't give me that," Perce said rudely. "I know Ed Pringle – went to school with him, in fact. He has a head of bushy hair. You don't."

Nothing would convince Perce that this man was Ed. "I knew the whole family," he said. "I know his mother's house. It's empty now because she died. If you were Ed Pringle you'd have hair and you'd be living in your mother's house."

Ed had been away in No-Hair Land for five months or so, and he hadn't heard about his mother. "Poor mum," he cried.

He went to live in her old house and got a big happy tongue-hanging-out dog called Pongo. But except for

Pongo, no one would talk to him. Even the grocery boy wouldn't deliver Ed's favourite meat pies, so he had to eat sausages.

Now it's a well known fact that news travels mysteriously. Ed Pringle had friends back in No-Hair Land, and the news that Ed had found a nice house to live in spread in no time. One no-hair person realised that he too could travel to the other side of the mountain and find a nice house, so off he went. After that, others got the same idea and soon there were quite a few of them living in Bushy-Hair Town.

This would make Perce Mullens mad. He would run out his back door shouting at anyone with no hair – including people who were merely bald but still had their regular body hair, which of course Perce couldn't see. No one took him seriously. They laughed at him, so one day he went home and got his gun.

His wife followed him out onto the porch, saying, as she often did, "Perce, don't be such an ass. Get back here in the house. Stop making a fool of yourself. That pistol's not loaded anyway."

"A fool of myself, is it? I'll show you!" He dropped the pistol, which *was* loaded, and it went off with a bang. This made him even madder. He took the ride-on lawn mower out onto the street and tried to run over no-hair people.

But they were too nimble and jumped out of his way, laughing because none of them had ever seen anyone get mad before. They shouted for joy, saying, "Oh, great master. Do it again!"

Perce ran back to his house to get the washing machine but Mrs Mullens was too quick for him. She shoved him into the laundry saying, "Now calm down, Perce. I won't unlock the door until you do."

Still, Bushy-Hair Town kept filling up with no-hair people, who had no idea they were doing anything wrong. Just walking around with no hair was bad enough, and then they started climbing in through open windows and up empty chimneys and even into front parlours. Some were even hanging out of side windows.

The people of Bushy-Hair Town started to become anxious and lock their front gates; then they bolted their verandas, their front doors, and their back doors. "Something has to be done to make these no-hairs behave like civilised human beings," they said.

So someone set up a large tent for training no-hair people. The main idea was that they should grow hair, starting where it could be seen. It worked – after a lot of fines were imposed.

A bit later Perce Mullens, who had lost most of his wife's furniture by throwing it at the hated no-hair people, met Ed Pringle in the street. Ed's hair had grown back by then.

Perce stopped dead and cried, "Ed Pringle! Boy, am I glad to see you. There's been some galoot with no hair pretending to be you. He couldn't fool me! But anyway, Ed, it's great to see you. How've you been? I hear your mother died. Gee, I'm sorry. Well, I'll be off. You know I'm chief of the Boy Scouts campaign against them no-hair invaders? We're making progress. Trained ten of them yesterday. They've agreed to grow hair. Well, so long. Glad you're back!"

After listening politely to this long speech, Ed went back home to his mother's house and sat down for a beer and a smoke. "It's a crazy world, Pongo," he said to his big happy tongue-hanging-out dog. Ψ

Illustration: Drawing by Eileen Kramer, 2020.

198

Mr Evolution

Molly and My-Lin had been teenage friends. For a while they had lived together — that is to say, Molly, having nowhere to live, came to live with My-Lin and her mother. They also worked together in an odd sort of job that Molly considered offered no future prospects.

Molly's aim was to make enough money to buy her own house with three bedrooms, a lounge room and other necessary rooms, as well as a good front lawn and a long backyard. She had faith it would happen even though she didn't know how.

My-Lin had her own ideas about the future. Her interest was in the plight of humanity and beyond that, the world, the planets and the universe. And God — especially the puzzle of who created Him. At first this was not very pressing. She referred to evolution as if that strange force of nature was a person: Mr Evolution. She had great faith that he would one day reveal everything.

"If you're so interested in those things (she meant the planets and the universe)," Molly told her, "you should take science at the university." She didn't say 'uni' because she liked full and proper names.

My-Lin didn't go to the university because she had confidence in her own way of learning. She said she had met some people who went to the university and still didn't know anything.

One day she took Molly to lunch in a cafe close to where they worked, and a girl sat down at their table because there wasn't room anywhere else.

My-Lin was talking about the universe in an imaginative way, and after a while the girl said, "Oh, why don't you get into the real world?"

"What?" said My-Lin, a bit surprised. She looked hard at the girl and added, in a strong voice: "You wouldn't know the real world if it hit you on your head."

Thank goodness the girl had finished her lunch by then. She got up and left Molly and My-Lin to themselves

"She was very rude," Molly said.

"I know lots of people like that," My-Lin said. "But there's no such thing as the real world."

Molly looked doubtful: she believed her dream house was in a real world. "People like that wouldn't understand you," she said. "I still think, though, that you should take science. You'd be able to express your ideas in …" She searched for a real word for 'the real world'.

But My-Lin still went on in her own way.

Molly eventually got her dream house. She also got married to a nice young man named Trevor. They loved each other quite a lot – more than people who get married just because they like each other. They had three children so the three bedrooms were just right.

Unfortunately, Trevor could not stand the stress of the real world, and he took to the Drink. Molly couldn't stand that. She nagged a bit too much and only made things worse. Yet the bond of love was strong so they stayed together.

My-Lin didn't get married. She had one great romance but that didn't include marriage. She went on thinking about the universe and the planets and how Mr Evolution would fix everything.

Meanwhile, the real world went on, with all its troubles and some great things too, like music and dance and theatre and babies being born – all the usual things. People selling their big homes and moving into smaller apartments and flats. New discoveries of treatments for cancer, and good new movies, as well as better care for the elderly. There were many other things too.

My-Lin was rather pleased with Mr Evolution, and decided to write a story about the future for a competition with a $1000 prize.

Five thousand years from now, according to My-Lin's story, there would be no more pain and strife. People would have lost their troublesome bodies, and their spirits would be housed in wispy but beautiful fabric that never had to be laundered. Their houses would be made of removable see-through material that could be found anywhere in forests (forests still existed). People no longer had to eat to keep themselves alive; they no longer had to kill for food. Mr Evolution had invented a new part of the body that absorbed protein and vitamins from the air so they ate as they breathed.

The sexes didn't need each other like they used to. Women were self-multiplying in a less painful way. Men had been transformed into bee-like drone workers who could put up a cobwebby kind of dwelling for you within half an hour – and not charge for it, as the monetary system no longer existed.

All unnecessary stone brick and steel buildings had simply crumbled away and electricity was no longer necessary as most people could turn on their own inner light.

Mr Evolution had fixed all that.

Then one day, My-Lin came upon God idling His time away beside a sacred spring. He was supposed to be holding a party but it wasn't much of one: nothing to eat, no drinks and no cigarette smoke. Nearby was Mr Evolution looking like God's right-hand man.

"Hello My-Lin," said God. "I know it's not much, but I can't resist a sacred spring. In your time and space, it's coffee shops all over the place. Here it's sacred springs everywhere. I can't resist them."

My-Lin felt she had to say something. "Oh, my Lord," she began. But He stopped her and said, "Call me 'God' – that's my name for goodness sake."

She felt rebuked and almost forgot what she had to say, but ploughed on anyway. "Oh God, you were supposed to have created the whole universe, but Mr Evolution has done such a good job!"

He interrupted her again. "I know, but I'll just wait another million years until it's time to create it again. Don't worry about that, My-Lin."

My-Lin could see poor Trevor the Drunkard sitting on

God's left side, with a silly smile on his face. And there was Molly seated on God's right side, wishing she could get across to help her husband. She was a good woman, My-Lin thought, so she asked God, would He please put things right with Trevor if there was to be another time around for the creation.

Then everyone except God himself disappeared. It was quiet, and there was nothing but blue sky and white clouds.

My-Lin's story won the $1000 prize, and she took Molly away for a trouble-free weekend somewhere in the Gulf of Carpentaria.

"It's alright, Molly," she said. "I've spoken to God. He's going to make things right with Trevor." Ψ

Illustration: Collage by Eileen Kramer using a photograph of her dancing in 'Osiris and the Black Hole', Lewisburg West Virginia.

had something w...
...ght and the Nile. As
...s one idea gave birth
...other idea and chally...
...ised a scene with me...
...s, even though they had
lower parts.
the camels, of course, w...
...ted. They, poor guys,
...y realised they had n...
and back legs.
...Shelly tidied them...
...had new costumes +
...em. I didn't mend w...

Behind the stories

Eileen's stories can be enjoyed simply for what they are. But in many cases she has woven her tale around real experiences and real people, and because she has led such a full, creative – and yes, long – life, readers may also be interested in some context.

The following pages provide a very brief biographical overview, along with her own comments on each story. 'Essential Eileen' on page 220 offers some leads for further exploration.

Sydney – Cremorne and Coogee: 1914–1935

Born in 1914, Eileen grew up in Cremorne, a child of the bush and the harbour. When her parents separated in 1927, she moved with her mother and brother to the beachside suburb of Coogee, where "Edward and I spent most of our time surfing and sunbathing", and her friend Betty came to live with them. In 1933, at the age of 19, Eileen began to learn singing and piano from a local teacher and, two years later, she became a student at the Conservatorium of Music on Macquarie Street, paying for her tuition by working as an usherette in a small movie house.

Left: With my mother and brother Edward, c. 1917.

The stories

A lucky dog, page 47: A true story, of my mother's mother and her bricklayer beau, and the adventures of Flossy the dog.

Kisses, page 135: Also a true story, although names have been changed. My friend Betty and her beau Perry Saunders also play rather more fantastical roles as Molly and Trevor in the story *Mr Evolution*.

Sydney – Phillip Street: 1936–1939

Eileen was 22 when she went to live in a rooming house around a courtyard in Phillip Street. It was a bohemian life. "Imagine, if one were interested in the arts, living in the centre of Sydney. And if that were not enough, throw in the Botanic Gardens and the Domain and the NSW Art Gallery... All this was our front garden. For five shillings a week."

Above: Rediscovering the stuffed body of the tortoise we used to visit in the Botanic Gardens.

Right: With boyfriend Richard Want, a psychoanalyst who lived and worked around the corner in Macquarie Street.

The stories

The rat, page 97: I did once knock an unfortunate rat out of my bathroom window, and I did sometimes have dinner at a restaurant called 'The Spotted Dog' that had lost its 'S'. But the rest of this story comes from my imagination.

Sex & grammar, page 185: The seed for this story was a memory of something I saw one day walking to the Art Gallery through the Domain. Two old people (probably only in their 60s!) were sitting on a park bench kissing. This was a revelation to me as I had thought sexual desire ended at about the age of 35! I continued on my way in a state of wonder.

The tortoise, page 89: There really was a tortoise living in the Botanic Gardens in the 1930s. I used to visit her regularly. Her body is now on display in a glass case in one of the offices of the Gardens. When I saw her again in 2018, she was wearing an undignified-looking party hat, which made me a bit sad.

The Bodenwieser years: 1940–1953

Eileen first saw the Bodenwieser Dance Company perform in 1940, at the age of 25. "Whatever it was in my psyche that recognises its own told me immediately that this was for me. The next day I found out where Madame Bodenwieser was teaching and went there straightaway to see whether I could become a student of the dance." By the end of 1940, she was given her first solo, 'Spring', and was designing costumes for the company as well. Her first performance as a professional member of the company was in 1943.

Jean Raymond and I in 'Waterlilies', 1947

The stories

The horse, page 83: Sometimes you have a bunch of images which seem unconnected. If you were a knitter, you might knit them, with the magic of numbers, into an exotic sweater or shawl. If you were a writer or a dancer, you might weave them into such a story as *The horse*. The images here are: Madame, leader of a dance troupe; two of her dancers, one of whom is my dear friend Jean; Percival Savage, who I introduce in the story *A sad monkey* and who inspired the strange Mr Low; a Chinese temple; shadow dancers of the temple; and a lovely white horse.

Angels, page 115: This is pretty much a true story, including getting high on fumes while painting toy animals.

Left: *In the social pages: Sydney Morning Herald, 18 June 1953.*

Note the spelling of Eileen's family name as 'Cramer' here. Her father had changed it to the non-German version during WW1, and Eileen retained this spelling for her creative work until the 1980s.

Right: *Performing 'Indian Love Song', c.1952. Noel Rubie Pty Ltd.*

The company toured extensively in Australia, as well as New Zealand, South Africa, and India. Photo is from New Zealand tour, 1947. Left to right: (Back row) Coralie Hinkley, Shona Dunlop, Hilary Napier, Doreen Tooley; (2nd row) Jean Raymond, Dora Stern; (3rd row) Margaret Chapple, Anne Pitsch; (front row) Elizabeth Russell, Eileen Cramer, Mardi Watchorn. behind Elizabeth Russell is Frederic McCallum (Tour Manager).

209

India: 1953–56

"I lived in India for quite a long time, I danced there...and it gave me a purpose. I wasn't just wandering about looking at things. I absorbed a lot in India." Eileen danced at the Taj Hotel in Mumbai, and in New Delhi, and at the Metropole Hotel in Karachi, where she was also commissioned to paint wall murals in various areas of the hotel.

At the Metropole Hotel, Karachi, with one of my wall murals, 'Scenes of Paris'.

Two paintings inspired by my time in India and Pakistan: 'Dancer in the Palace, Delhi' and 'Women and Sheep, Karachi'.

The stories

The crow, page 77: With the odours of jasmine and garbage, and the heat and cool waters of the Bay of Mumbai down below, the terrace of the Taj Hotel is an experience to remember. But beware of the crows at afternoon tea time.

210

Paris and London: 1957 – early 60s

Eileen spent the late 1950s and early 60s in Paris and London, as well as travelling on the Continent. She worked as an artist's model – "I liked the stillness of it, and the two-minute poses were like 'frozen dance'."

Travelling in Spain with Jane Blake, my companion in 'The earthworm'.

The well-connected Percival Savage in London. He was very kind to me when I first arrived in Paris.

The stories

The earthworm, page 11: All true. You never know what you will see on the way to the Côte d'Azur. And you can find out more about the Claux family online if you're interested.

A sad monkey, page 17: I wish it were otherwise, but in truth I have no idea what happened to the sad monkey Percival and I met in a flea market in Paris. Perhaps someone really did rescue him in the end.

The artist's model, page 125: What happened to Lucy Bower in Soho also happened to me. London was an exciting place to be in the 1960s.

Tea on the ward, page 141: Similarly, Celine, the heroine of this story, might in fact be me. I have not been able to find any historical mentions of Gracie Fields' tea-time bequest but I was certainly a beneficiary at the time.

211

New York – East 91st Street: 1960s

In New York Eileen lived and worked for many years with Polish-American filmmaker Baruch Shadmi, whom she had met in Paris. Together, they made The Pilgrimage of Truth, *a feature-length 35mm morality tale combining live action and stop motion shot mainly in their apartment. "For five years, we gave it all our attention and creative energy."*

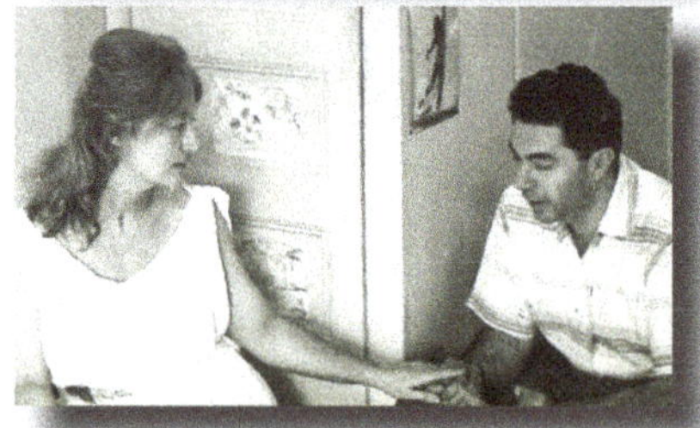

Top: *Painting 'Song of Songs' – Hava Nagila – for a New York restaurant.*

Bottom: *With Baruch in our apartment.*

Above: *Baruch saw me at work one day, modelling a small white figurine. It was the Figure of Truth, from Madame's dance drama, 'The Pilgrimage of Truth'. I was not sure what I would do with it. I might never have made it had I not happened to have some fine white paper and a jar of Elmer's glue. When I explained who the figure was supposed to be, he surprised me by saying, 'We could make an animated film of that story.' So we did.*

The stories

The cat, page 37: Jill and Ruben in this story are essentially me and Baruch. PussPuss was indeed a very special cat – it turned out she was actually a male whose sexual parts had never descended. She played a big role in our lives. I was very sad when she died while I was away on a visit to Sydney.

212

New York – West 57th Street: 1968–1987

In 1968, Eileen moved out of the apartment she had shared with Baruch, although she still spent almost every weekend with him and continued to help him with his creative projects. "I no longer thought of myself as a dancer. My life was completely bound to his." Baruch died in 1987, and six months later, Eileen took a train to Lewisburg, West Virginia.

Above: *Posing for the Art Students League.*
Right: *In my friend Dagmar Barsh's flat, West 57th Street, NY, around the time I met Gloria Swanson at Tiffany's glove counter.*

The tiger, page 69: Although set in India and inspired by a real drive from Mumbai to Goa, *The tiger* comes from my time in New York in the 1960s and 70s. Arriving in Manhattan in the height of Women's Lib, I was made aware of the main reasons for women's discontent and resentment. That is what *The tiger* is about.

The glove counter, page 149: I loved living in West 57th Street, and it's true that I met Gloria Swanson when I was trying on gloves at Tiffany's. Lunch at the Russian Tea Room with her might have stretched the friendship though!

213

From *Australian Women's Weekly*, 5 December 1962

NIGHTFALL: NEW YORK

● On the night the Cuban crisis seemed most tense, Australian Eileen Cramer, artist, dancer, model, and costume designer, saw the sun set from the roof of New York's Flat-Iron Building, the city's first skyscraper of 20 storeys.

We have published two amusing feature stories by Eileen — about an apartment in Paris and, more recently, about her visit to a Paris fashion house. But the tense and emotional atmosphere of New York on that night prompted her to write . . .

● Skyline of Lower Manhattan, the island Eileen Cramer refers to.

*Last night I saw sunset
from the roof.
Flaming, beautiful —
the deep red was reflected
in the waters of the Hudson —
on the funnels
of the ships.*

*This was a backdrop of nature,
behind the diamond lights
of the city set in squares,
cut in squares, with
long straight streams of
light in the streets.*

*I was lonely.
A stranger was I.
Two sheets of newspaper in the sky
swooped and dived above me
in the wind.
Two helicopters flew
in a straight line towards
the end of the Island.*

*All cities are beautiful at night
seen from a high place.
Flaming sky is glorious
in times of peace.
But one wonders where God has
   gone
when men fear,
and shout for war.*

*Down in the street, a woman
with a stick clung to a post
and waited for the lights to change.
I started off, then looked back
and took her arm,
Together we crossed Broadway.
"I'll be all right now,"
she said, and went her way.*

*All day long voices come to us on
the radio. Noble sentiments abound,
and fill the people with
Fear;
Some cry out for violent action,
some beg the President
to call the blockade off.*

*Between the bulletins,
two composers
chatter happily.
They tell each other tales of
music — what Debussy said that
famous night, when "Melisande"
was first performed . . .
what Wagner said, at some rehearsal
. . . in Berlin.*

*I ask myself, am I a coward?
Is it only because I am
separated from the one I love
that I feel so afraid? It's not
I want to run away so much,
as that I want to run back
to him.*

*I am in my bed. I am warm
and hardly awake. I am still
alive, deliciously drowsy, and I think
how wonderful it is
to have a room, this bed, and the
morning coffee in a minute.*

*I love the bed, and when I get up
there will be a bath and clothes
to put on.
I will go to the letter-box, to look
for a letter. I will take up the pen
to write.
I am home, and need not wander
over the ravished earth, breathing
poisoned air, and stepping over
the bodies of the dead.
They say there is a chance
it will not happen. We will
squeeze through this time.
But has it frightened us enough
to make us think?*

Writing as 'Eileen Cramer', Eileen had many articles published in the Australian Women's Weekly during the 1960s and 70s. Search the National Library's Trove database at https://trove.nla.gov.au/newspaper/

West Virginia – Powley's Creek: Summers 1980s

Before she moved to West Virginia in 1988, Eileen spent several summers there working on playwright Maryat Lee's Eco Theatre projects. Maryat had been a good friend and mentor to Eileen even before she had arrived in New York from Paris.

Rehearsing for the Eco Theatre production of John Henry, legendary black tunnel digger.

Maryat Lee – accepted by the locals because she was a descendant of General Robert E Lee.

The stories

The goat, page 23: A true account of my time at the Women's Farm with Maryat and the Eco Theatre.

The skunk, page 43: An homage to the Powley's Creek community and my friends Beth White and Chally Erb – the Ronnie and Foster of this story.

Fireflies, page 65: On one of my visits from New York, with my cat, I had an experience of the great 'ooomm' just like this.

The camels, page 31: Based on my work with the Trillium Performing Arts Collective. Everyone knows the theatre is a fantasy world, and there's no law saying the camels should stay locked up in the props room.

The bees, page 3: This is a fairy tale and doesn't need any explanation, except that it was inspired by West Virginia. The two houses are real too, and so was Bill. Mr B is a

216

West Virginia – Hinton and Lewisburg: 1988 to 2013

In Lewisburg Eileen met sixth-generation West Virginian Bill Tuckwiller. Love blossomed. Eileen rediscovered dance, contributing her choreography, costume design and performance skills to the Trillium Performing Arts Collective until she returned to Australia in 2013.

Top: *The Tuckwiller house in Lewisburg.*
Bottom: *Trillium garden party performance.*

Bill Tuckwiller and I, sometime in the 1990s. We were together until Bill's death in 1997.

mysterious character in some way connected to the bees. And some bees do make their hives in the ground (or so it is said).

The garden party, page 177: A story about me/Eva meeting Bill /James and going to live with him.

The mouse, page 61: In Bill's garden. Ingredients: a house, a garden, a young woman, an umbrella, two cats and one tiny mouse. Weave them together and you have a story about a helpless little creature faced with death, suddenly saved by fate.

Dogs & cats, page 55: Not about West Virginia, but about a trip to Italy soon after I had moved in with Bill – to visit friends I had met years ago in Karachi. The story of their dogs and cats provided a good excuse to remember the visit.

Australia: 2013 to present

Since returning to Australia aged 99, Eileen has been prolific. She has produced two dance dramas for the stage and collaborated with filmmaker Sue Healey on another. She has also published a book of stories, performed in a stage play, a TV series and music videos, and presented workshops at two major dance festivals. The 2020 COVID-19 lockdown saw her writing the stories that became this book as well as conceiving a new work for film.

The stories

A feisty dog, page 51: Dear Tilly. Memories of her and Barbara made me think about how I came back to Australia after so many years.

Actors, page 155: The true story of a trip to Queensland with my friend Tracey Spring to play a role in the TV series *The End* (See-Saw Films, 2019). I wonder if Jimmy will ever read it?

The man, page 121: When I saw the photograph of my friend Sue Healey's husband standing in the doorway of the James Turrell installation in Canberra this story jumped right out of my head and onto the page.

The resident, page 163: A true story with no ending. We still have to see his face, and it's not likely to happen because he's on the second floor and I'm on the first! Maybe when the coronavirus lockdown is over...

Room 8, page 171: An account of a day at Lulworth House, where I met Susan and saw the picture that solved the problem of what to use to illustrate *A sad monkey*.

The tower, page 109, and *Mr Evolution, page 199*, are stories from nowhere and anywhere.

And *Elephants*, who knows? A story that may well come true some day!

At Brickfields Cafe, Chippendale, 2013.

'The Early Ones', 2015 (Saeed Khan AFP).

In Sue Healey's 'Now Memory', 2017.

'The Buddha's Wife', 2017 (RVG Lighting).

Sketching on the veranda at Lulworth House, 2018 (ABC News: Nicole Chettle).

Masks I have made for my latest work-in-progress, October 2020.

Essential Eileen

www.eileen-kramer.com

Books

Eileen: Tales from the Phillip Street Courtyard, Eileen Kramer and Tracey Spring, Melbourne Books, 2018

Walkabout Dancer, Eileen Kramer, Trafford Publishing, 2008: A memoir including fascinating accounts of the Bodenwieser years, Eileen's travels in India and Europe, and her time in New York and then West Virginia.

The Heliotropians, Eileen Kramer, Trafford Publishing, 2009: A fantasy novel following the adventures of a group of young time travellers.

Interviews

Eileen Kramer interviewed by Michelle Potter [sound recording]: Oral history, National Library of Australia, 2003
https://trove.nla.gov.au/work/22346077?

Articles

'The Creative Life of Eileen Kramer,' photoessay by Kylie Melinda Smith, *Griffith Review 68: Getting On*, Text Publishing 2020

'Bohemian rhapsody', Fenella Souter, *Sydney Morning Herald Good Weekend*, 3 November 2018. https://www.smh.com.au/national/bohemian-rhapsody-why-there-s-no-stopping-this-103-year-old-dancer-20181030-p50ctl.html

Video

Video portrait of Eileen by Sue Healey: https://vimeo.com/244582079

One plus one, interview with Jane Hutcheon, ABC, 20 December 2018
https://www.abc.net.au/news/programs/one-plus-one/2018-12-20/one-plus-one:-eileen-kramer/10640714?nw=0

Spotlight on Australian Ballet, National Film Board, 1948. National Film and Sound Archive of Australia. Watch at: https://youtu.be/ky9i9aRh-Y4 [Eileen dances in 'Waterlilies' from 13:47, and in 'Demon Machine' and then 'The Blue Danube' from 22:05]

*Eileen wearing a hat she designed and made as part of a promotion for
the Australian Wool Board, 1947*

Editor's epilogue

When I began working with Eileen in January 2020, the task seemed relatively straightforward: to transcribe a few stories she had written, read them back for her to check, then hand over the transcription. It turned to be rather more interesting than that!

Eileen is a natural storyteller, and for me as an editor it has been truly rewarding to spend time with her, helping these tales of hers to find their best shapes. She knows what she wants, but also when to let go of something that hasn't quite come off. And she allowed me to have some fun with the illustrations too.

Eileen's creativity is her being and her purpose. Wherever she is, whatever her circumstances, at five years old or a hundred and five, there is always something that sparks her interest, ignites her imagination – an ember she will want to breathe into being. That does not mean there is no discipline or rigour in each endeavour. Quite the opposite. It is 'work'. But it is also 'life'.

This makes her inspiring to be around. She has taught me – and continues to teach me – much about the importance of creativity and purpose, especially during that strange, somehow introspective, 'year of the virus'. And I think I have shown her that working with an editor is less about 'fixing' things and more a kind of midwifery for the imagination, helping to bring her stories into the world, robust and kicking and ready to meet their readers – just in time for her 106th birthday!

It has been a privilege to be part of this process and I thank Eileen, so full of wit and wisdom and adventures from a life richly lived, for recognising the value of inviting a friend into the delivery room.

Catherine Gray
November 2020

From Eileen's latest dance film, *The God Tree*,
in production during 2021. (Photo: Richard Corfield)
Find out more at eileen-kramer.com